SEE YOU AGAIN

An Accidental Pregnancy Book

Rin Sher

Copyright © 2021 RIN SHER

All rights reserved

The characters and events portrayed in this book are fictitious. Any similarity to real persons, living or dead, is coincidental and not intended by the author.

No part of this book may be reproduced, or stored in a retrieval system, or transmitted in any form or by any means, electronic, mechanical, photocopying, recording, or otherwise, without express written permission of the publisher.

ISBN-:9798546772444

Cover design by: Art Painter
Library of Congress Control Number: 2018675309
Printed in the United States of America

*To those who think you can't,
you can.*

CONTENTS

Title Page
Copyright
Dedication
CHAPTER ONE	1
CHAPTER TWO	12
CHAPTER THREE	29
CHAPTER FOUR	34
CHAPTER FIVE	41
CHAPTER SIX	47
CHAPTER SEVEN	54
CHAPTER EIGHT	64
CHAPTER NINE	72
CHAPTER TEN	79
CHAPTER ELEVEN	86
CHAPTER TWELVE	93
CHAPTER THIRTEEN	103
CHAPTER FOURTEEN	112
CHAPTER FIFTEEN	122
CHAPTER SIXTEEN	129
CHAPTER SEVENTEEN	138
CHAPTER EIGHTEEN	146

CHAPTER NINETEEN	160
CHAPTER TWENTY	166
CHAPTER TWENTY-ONE	173
CHAPTER TWENTY-TWO	184
CHAPTER TWENTY-THREE	195
EPILOGUE	204
Thank You!	209
Books By This Author	211
CONTACT	215

CHAPTER ONE

Jasper

I watch as the tenth water droplet slides slowly down the side of my glass, landing in the pool at the bottom with the rest of the accumulated water. The sound of happy patrons surrounds me while I sit alone at the bar, staring at my glass.

I don't feel depressed exactly, just... weird. Odd. Earlier today was my brother Lance's funeral. If we were closer and I'd seen him more than three times in the past five years, I might feel differently. But him being twelve years older than me meant that he was off living his life long before I grew up. He had moved across the country before I even knew what an erection was, and I got my first facial hair.

Needless to say, Trent was more like an acquaintance to me than an actual brother. I still feel the loss, in a way. Knowing that he's no longer in the world doesn't feel right, regardless of how close or not we were.

Seeing how distraught my parents have been for the past few days hasn't felt good either. It's no secret that he was their favorite. I was more of an afterthought. A mistake. They had me later in life when they thought they were done already, so I never saw them as the fun-loving, energetic parents that my friends had or what my brother had likely grown up with. Instead, I got the no-nonsense, tired, and 'don't bother me' parents that didn't show me any affection. They were pretty strict as well. I wasn't often allowed to go play with my friends.

I'm not complaining. They were good to me in a way. I'm sure I would have turned out a lot differently otherwise. I like to think I have a good head on my shoulders. For a few years, I focused on my medical studies, intending to be a doctor, but then I switched to training to be a Sonographer when I realized that that was something I was more interested in doing instead. My parents never said anything about me making the switch, so I choose to think they were fine with it rather than them not caring at all.

I started out with Vascular Sonography but recently changed over to Obstetrics. There aren't a lot of men in that field, but that doesn't really bother me, and I enjoy it nonetheless.

My brother, on the other hand? He was a freelance real estate agent. The talk-to-everyone-he-meets type of person. Wild. Outgoing. Loud.

I'm the quiet one. Not very social. Mild. The son whom my mother swore up and down had Aspergers the whole time I was growing up and yet refused to have me tested. I did go for testing as soon as I was old enough to go on my own, though. It turns out I'm just somewhat shy and don't talk much.

When I left to go to college, Lance moved back here to be

closer to my parents again. It's like we did a brother swap. When he was gone, I lived here with them, and when I moved away, he moved back.

I down the rest of my drink and signal the bartender for another. I'm only in town for one more night, and I didn't want to spend it at my parent's house. It's filled with friends of the family and other family members from out of town, mourning and talking non-stop about a person who I hardly knew.

He had made friends with the whole town, which is probably why his funeral was so big.

I guess that's perhaps where the weird feelings come from, or maybe it's guilt. Because *everyone else* knew him so well, and now, I'll never have the chance to get to know him at all. I feel guilty that I never tried before it was too late. I guess he didn't either, but he's not the one left.

The bartender hands me another drink right as the sound of girlish laughter hits my ears, and then a body thumps into my back, almost causing my drink to spill everywhere.

"Oh my goodness, I'm *so* sorry," a voice says. "My friend has had a bit too much to drink. Knocked me right into you."

"That's okay," I respond before I've even seen the owner of the beautiful voice.

When my eyes finally do land on her, I'm kind of thrown back a little. I don't know what I was expecting, but it sure as hell wasn't her. Bright blue eyes with a twinkle in them shine in my direction, accompanied by a wide smile just as bright. Waves of lush dark hair hang down over her shoulder, reaching the hem of her top. She is by far the most beautiful woman in here.

I had taken a peek around the bar when I first arrived and had noticed her immediately with a group of other women.

"Come on, *Ann*, let's get you to the ladies' room." She grabs hold of her friend, leading her away to the restrooms on the right.

My eyes linger on her, watching as she walks away. I can't seem to tear them away. The rest of her body matches perfectly with her face, and the curve of her ass looks incredible in those tight jeans. The dip of her waist in the body-hugging top she's wearing begs for my hands to be there, gripping tightly as I thrust in.

Shit. I swallow the dryness in my throat.

When did I last stare at a woman like this?

When did I last have such thoughts like that?

I trail my eyes back up to the back of her head in time to see her glance over her shoulder at me, giving another smile. It's the type that's a mixture of sexy and friendly curiosity. I hold her gaze briefly before turning away, waiting until she's not looking in my direction anymore before returning my attention back to her.

The second she disappears through the door, a form of guilt appears in my gut. I shouldn't be gazing at a woman like that after being at a funeral today. I shouldn't be checking her out while all the people in my family are grieving.

"I was just looking," I mumble to myself. Then I twist on my stool so that I'm now facing the rest of the room instead of the bottles of alcohol on the wall.

It's busy here in the hotel bar, but not too crowded. A group of guys are over by the pool tables, cheering every once in a while at a game playing silently on the TVs. An assortment of people are on the makeshift dance floor, moving their bodies to the beat. And most of the booths are filled with different groups of people just having a good time. A particularly noisy group of women take up the biggest booth at the other end of the room, which is where I first saw the beautiful brunette.

"So I have this thing," a sweet voice beside me says. "That when you feel a certain spark or connection with someone, you should see what it's about. You should at least talk to the person."

I slowly turn my head to see the beautiful woman from a few minutes ago leaning on the bar, wearing a soft smile. Her attention is solely on me, so I'm guessing the remark was aimed at me. I'm not quite sure what to say to her, so I end up just staring. There's probably a ridiculous blank look on my face.

"Do *you* feel it?" she asks, leaning forward into my space, flicking her gaze between my eyes.

I feel the urge to shift on my stool as heat touches the tips of my ears. She's so close. Close enough that I can smell her despite being surrounded by the scent of alcohol. She smells *good.* I'm not sure if it's perfume, her shower gel, or what, but it's having a weird effect on my senses.

"Um." That's the only word that I manage to get out.

She moves back, giving me space to breathe again. Then, tilting her head to the side, she says, "Oh yeah, you feel it."

Riley

My heart pitter-patters away in my chest as I hold his gaze. I don't know where this boldness is coming from. It's not that I'm a particularly shy person or anything, but saying something like that to a stranger is new to me, and I haven't even had a single drop of alcohol tonight, despite the fact that my table is probably full of the drunkest people in here.

The guy gives me a small smile, but it's almost as if he's not used to doing it and is unsure how to react. "How do you know?" he finally asks.

My eyes are on his pink lips as he speaks, and it takes me a moment to realize he asked a question. I shrug. "I can just tell."

I've actually been watching this handsome stranger for most of the night. He's been alone the entire time and has barely looked around. He hasn't even spoken a word to anyone but the bartender. That is, he hadn't until my friend Chelsea stumbled and caused me to crash right into him. Though it was brief, I saw something in his dark brown eyes when he looked at me, and it was like fate had led me to him via Chelsea. He intrigued me, but I knew I needed to come back and talk to him without a drunk friend hanging off my arm.

Which reminds me...I glance over at the booth full of my friends to make sure Chelsea made it back okay, and...yep, there she is. When I turn back to the mystery man, I notice he's looking at me with curiosity.

"What?" I ask.

He shakes his head and looks away almost sheepishly.

"So, what's your name?" I ask.

"Jasper."

I pick up the hand he had resting on his thigh to shake. "Nice to meet you, Jasper."

His hand feels so...I guess the best way to describe it would be *manly*. It's big, strong, and warm. And it has that natural roughness to it that seems to be normal for men.

While my hand continues its hold on his, I try to think of what to tell him. Do I give him my actual name? Or do I stick to the middle-name rule my friends and I have been holding to for the past few days?

Ah, screw it. If I'm never seeing him again, then it doesn't matter. Middle name it is.

"Shay," I reply as I give his hand a little squeeze.

"Shay." He repeats the name like he's trying it out on his tongue. "It's nice to meet you, too."

Knowing that I'll never see him again is giving me a sort of confidence that I maybe wouldn't normally have. It's the reason why I haven't let go of his hand, and it's the reason why I lean in once again and say, "You have really nice eyes."

They're a deep brown color, almost black, and they stare intensely back at me before roaming over my face. He's the very definition of tall, dark, and handsome, but he doesn't have the cockiness I'd expect to go along with his good looks. I find it more attractive than if he were to be strutting around like a peacock with his feathers out like some of the guys here. He has a quiet confidence that speaks louder to me than the person singing off-key a few seats down from us.

"So do you," he replies, reminding me that I'm *still* leaning in and my hand is *still* in his.

Moving back out of his space and releasing his hand, I finally take a seat on the stool next to his, facing out towards the room like he is.

"Are you from around here?" I ask, leaning my elbows along the bar behind me. Even though *I'm* not from around here, and I'm unfamiliar with the locals, he doesn't seem like he belongs here.

He shakes his head. "No."

"Me neither." I chew on my bottom lip as I try to think of what to say next. "Are you having a good night?"

"It's okay."

Some of my earlier confidence starts to waver when he doesn't make any effort to talk to me. Trying to get a conversation out of him is starting to feel like pulling teeth. Either he's not a big talker, or he's seriously not interested in having a conversation with me. I could have sworn I felt something when our eyes first locked. But maybe I'm just projecting what I wanted to feel.

These last few days with my girlfriends have been amazing. It's the last weekend before Mia, one of my best friends, gets married. We've been on a bachelorette weekend high. Every day has been filled with doing things that we usually wouldn't do. Case and point, me talking to a handsome stranger in this bar, well, trying to. I do really have a thing about taking action on gut feelings and instant connections, but I also wanted to continue with the theme of our trip.

This is also one of the last weekends that my girlfriends and I will be all together. Three of my friends will be moving away to continue on with their careers or simply for fresh starts elsewhere. Mia and I will be the only ones left, and she'll be married. Speaking of Mia, I watch as the bride-to-be makes her way toward me with a giant dopey smile.

"Whatcha doing, Shay-Shay?" she asks. Now I'm really glad I went with that name.

"I'm just talking to my new friend, Jasper, here." I gesture to him, and he lifts his glass up in a "hello" move.

"Hi," Mia says before discreetly widening her eyes at me. Even drunk, she never blurts out inappropriate or suggestive things like the other girls would. I love her for it. She won't ask me about him until we're somewhere completely private.

"What are you doing, Gail?" I ask Mia, using her middle name.

"I'm buying the girls another round of drinks," she answers, already sounding three sheets to the wind. "Are you sure you don't even want *one* drink?"

"Nah, I'm good, thanks." I've never been much of a drinker, and I would rather be able to keep an eye on all of the girls, getting them upstairs safely at the end of the night.

"Okay." She orders a tray full of shots and gives me a sloppy kiss on the cheek before leaving.

"Do you dance?" I ask Jasper once she's gone.

A small shake of his head. "No."

Okay then. "So, what brings you here?"

He lifts his glass again. "Just came for a drink."

Alright, now I officially feel like I've intruded on his night. He probably had a busy day and just wanted to come here and have a nice relaxing drink before he went up to his room, assuming he has a room in the hotel, and then I came along and bothered him.

"I'm sorry, you were probably enjoying your quiet time, and I interrupted it. I'll leave you to it."

I start to get up from the stool, but I'm stopped by his hand on my arm. "No. Please don't go. I'm sorry. I don't mean to be rude. I'm just not good at this. Not good at small talk."

My heart flutters a little as it does a little cheer at not being rejected. It's kind of endearing hearing him say that and seeing the look on his face. I guess my instincts didn't lead me astray after all. I settle back onto the stool again, turning my body a little more in his direction.

"Okay, let's skip the small talk then," I say. "If you could change just one thing in the world, what would it be?"

He actually chuckles softly at that, and it lightens his whole face. Every one of his features relaxes and softens as if the small laugh released a load of endorphins into him.

"Just straight into the deep end, huh?" He scratches at the

scruff on his jaw.

"Yep." I grin.

"Well, besides your first impression of me? I guess to make it so that no one gets sick anymore. You?"

"That is a really beautiful answer, Jasper," I tell him. "Hmm, let me think. I'd probably take away money."

He nods and looks as if he's contemplating my answer. "That sounds good as well...Shay." The sound of my name coming from his lips sends a shiver down my spine.

A moment later, the song changes to one of my favorites Mia and I always end up dancing to. I look over to the table and see that she's already getting up and waving at me to come onto the dance floor with her. I groan under my breath. If I don't go over there, she'll probably come and drag me.

"Are you sure you don't want to dance?" I ask Jasper. His face scrunches up in reply. "Okay, well, I'm being summoned by my friend, I'll just dance to this one, and then I'll be back."

I slide off the stool, giving a small smile over my shoulder as I walk away and hoping that maybe he'll change his mind and decide to follow. I can feel his eyes on me as I begin to move to the music, swaying my hips back and forth. A couple more girls join us, and then some guys from the pool tables make their way over as well.

I don't pay them any mind and close my eyes, losing myself in the song and dancing away. It's not even halfway through when I feel a presence behind me. Angling my head, I halt my movements and look up to see Jasper standing there. It causes a little thrill to shoot through me.

He's close, but he's not touching me, and I really want him to. So, I reach for his hand and place it on my hip, all while holding his gaze. Fingers press into my flesh as I slowly start to move again. Each swing of my hips has me shifting back until my back is pressed against his front. If this is as far as we go tonight, I will be completely content with that.

CHAPTER TWO

Jasper

Is this really happening? That's the thought that keeps circling through my mind while I lean in further, grinding my dick into her – trying to get as close as possible.

"I know this sounds cliché, and you may not believe me," I mumble as my lips slide along her jaw. "But I never do this."

"I do believe you, for some reason," she breathes. "And I don't do this either."

Her fingers trail up my neck, slipping through the strands of my hair, and the feeling of her lightly tugging at the ends has my eyes rolling back in pure ecstasy. The feeling is incredible.

"You like that, huh?"

"Mhmm," I hum before taking her mouth again.

Since this woman crashed into me earlier, my whole world has been tilted on its side. The quiet drink before returning to my quiet life has now somehow turned into bringing this beautiful woman, Shay, up to my room.

As soon as she started talking to me tonight, it was as if she suddenly breathed life into my solitary existence. It's hard to explain. I've had plenty of women talk to me before, but they usually take my lack of conversation skills as being an asshole or just not interested in them. I'm usually okay with that too, but with her, I *wanted* to talk to her. I wanted her to stay. Something in me snapped the second she started to get up and leave. I panicked. I couldn't let her walk away from me yet.

I match her kisses with the same fire and passion, and self-assurance that she has. I haven't felt those things in a long time, if ever.

I haven't particularly tried to have a relationship with anyone, and I really *don't* do one-night stands. But, god, there's something about this woman that has me losing control, and I *need* to have her.

Pulling her away from the wall just inside my hotel room, I lead her over to my king-size bed. "If you want to stop this, I completely understand. Whatever you want," I offer as I lay her down on the bed and then join her lying on my side.

"We probably should stop since this isn't normal for either of us."

I nod even as our lips join together again. My tongue sweeps into her mouth while hers moves to connect with mine. Her taste is addictive. I can't seem to get enough.

I manage to pry my mouth from hers long enough to say, "Yeah, we probably should." And then I slide my hands under the hem of her top, enjoying the feel of her warm, smooth skin beneath my fingertips.

"Okay, let's stop," she murmurs, only to reach for the button of my jeans.

In one swift motion, she undoes the button, pulls down the zipper, and then slides her hand in, grabbing hold of my throbbing dick. My breath stutters, and I let out a groan, stopping all of my movements for a moment while enjoying her stroking me. I don't even remember how long it's been since someone else's hand was on me.

After a pleasure-filled minute, I'm eager to resume my exploration of her body once again. There are too many clothes in the way, though, so I force her to release me so that I can undress her and then kiss each patch of skin I expose. Goosebumps appear following each touch of my lips, and I love that I'm able to give her that reaction.

Moving back off the bed, I stand up so that I can see her whole body better and admire the view. She looks beautiful and extremely appealing lying there naked on the bed in front of me. Perfect round breasts with pink nipples, slim waist, and curvy hips. I slowly undo the buttons of my shirt while trailing my eyes over her body, then toss it to the side. I notice her eyes widen when she looks up at me and realize she must be looking at the tattoos covering my chest and upper arms.

I don't blame her for being surprised. When I'm covered up, you can't tell that I have a single tattoo. They were my only form of rebellion when I went off to college, but I made sure they could be hidden. Her eyes roam over my chest before landing on my face again.

"Do you want to stop?" I ask.

She shakes her head slowly. "Take off your pants."

More than eager, I do as she says before returning to her side on the bed. I notice her licking her lips and her pupils dilating further when she finally slides her eyes down and sees my erection. And damn, if it doesn't make me feel good.

I try to take things slowly at first, ignoring my own wants and instead lavishing attention on her body, observing every inch, every curve. Kissing, touching, feeling.

But then she pushes me onto my back and straddles my hips without another word, driving me crazy as she slides her wet heat over my erection and her fingers splay over the ink on my chest.

"I love these," she says softly, trailing her fingers over one of the designs while still rubbing herself on me. "Do you have a condom?"

Shit, do I?

I haven't needed one in forever.

"There might be one...in my wallet...on the desk." I manage to get out while squeezing my eyes shut and digging my fingers dig into the flesh of her thighs because she's still sliding along the length of my dick, and it feels good, *really* good.

Pre-cum beads at my tip and then sticks to my stomach as she continues to move. I want to protest at the loss of contact when I feel her movements stop and a coolness replaces her body, but then she returns a moment later, holding a little foil packet. Thank goodness there was still one in there.

I go to take it from her, but she pulls it away. "Can I? I've never put one on before. And since this is a night of doing things we don't normally do..."

I lay back, clasping my hands behind my head, and watch as a smile spreads across her cheeks. God, I love that smile. I'd do just about anything to see it again and again.

She rips open the foil packet and then studies it to find the right side to roll down. Another groan rumbles through my chest when she grabs my shaft and sheathes it with the rubber. Once I'm completely covered, she lifts herself up and lines my dick up with her entrance.

I can't just lie, back not touching her, so I reach for her hips, digging my fingers in as she lowers herself down all the way. We're both still for a moment. Her adjusting to my size, and me relishing the feeling of being inside her and trying not to blow my load just yet.

After sucking in a deep breath, I lift her just slightly and bring her back down, just a small amount each time, until I know she's okay. Then I start thrusting at the same time that I bring her back down, harder and harder each time. It pulls a sexy moan from her throat.

"Yes," she hisses.

We continue on that way, but after a while, she takes over and starts moving herself up and down, faster and faster. Her breasts bounce in front of my face, begging to be licked. Lifting my head, I capture a nipple in my mouth and suck hard. Her bud hardens in my mouth, and I continue flicking my tongue around it. I feel her muscles clenching tighter in response. *Too* tight.

"Ohhhhh, Jasper," she cries out, swiveling her hips and grinding into me.

My pelvis goes into overdrive, trying to get as deep as possible, as fast as possible. The feeling of being surrounded by her heat is unbelievably gratifying.

She cries out again, throwing her head back and digging her nails into my shoulders as her orgasm ripples through her.

My movements get jerky as pleasure pools where we are joined and then begins to spread. "I'm going to come," I say through gritted teeth.

"Then come," Shay replies breathily.

She leans down and swirls her tongue over one of my nipples, and that's what does me in. My body stills deep inside her as I release everything I have into the condom, over and over.

When I finally open my eyes, Shay is slumped over me, and my arms are wrapped around her back, holding her close. "Wow," I say when I finally catch my breath.

"Yeah."

I loosen my arms when Shay shifts, trying to sit up. She slides off me to grab some tissues and then proceeds to remove the condom off my dick and throw it into the trash.

"Uh, thanks." I chuckle awkwardly.

"You're welcome." She smiles. "You look like you're kind of ruined."

"I feel like I am," I murmur. "In a good way."

She grins again and lays down against my chest, tracing her fingers lightly over my tattoos. My heartbeat finally settles after some time just lying with her.

"So, you're not from around here . . . What brings you here?" she asks eventually.

Unlike earlier, I feel like I can talk to her a little easier now that we've done *that*. "Well, actually, I *was* from here." I pause. "My brother's funeral was today. He drowned last week while he was drunk and hanging out with a bunch of women at the lake. He lived here with my parents."

She lifts her head off my chest to stare at me in shock and horror. "Oh my goodness. I'm so sorry. My mother died when I was a teenager, so if you want to talk about it, I'd be happy to listen."

"I'm sorry about your mom," I offer. "And it's okay. We weren't close *at all*. In fact, I hardly knew him. I couldn't tell you anything about him except what he looked like. I feel guilty for not feeling worse than I do, to be completely honest."

She quietly assesses me for a moment before speaking. "You know how some people who aren't related to you can become so close to you that they're like family?"

"Yes," I answer, while my fingers begin running through her soft hair.

"Well, the opposite can be said as well. Family can be like strangers, like people you're attached to for no other reason than you share DNA, just like my father... So don't feel too guilty."

I can't help but wonder what the story is about her father, but her tone and the way she said it doesn't seem like it's a subject she wants to talk about right now. "Well, you helped distract me for a while."

"There are actually a lot of articles that talk about how common it is for people to have sex after a funeral. It helps with grieving somehow."

"Really?"

"Mhmm."

I guess that makes sense in some weird way. People want to feel connected to those around them. Or feel alive.

We're both silent for a beat, me playing with her silky strands and her looking at my chest, studying my ink. I feel calm. I feel good, considering the day I had.

"What about you?" I ask. "You said you're not from around here?"

"No, it's my friend's bachelorette weekend. You saw my friends at the bar, the ones I danced with, and had to make sure they got to their rooms safely."

"Ah, yes."

Every now and then, after that song on the dance floor, one or two of them would drift over to see what Shay was doing while she was talking to me. All of them had smirks filled with insinuation on their heavily made-up drunk faces. Smirks that they tried and failed to hide.

"We decided that for something different, we'd go someplace that none of us had ever heard of."

"And Fairfield was the place?" I ask. "That doesn't surprise me."

"Yep," she replies. "We'll be here for another two days before leaving. The rest of the trip will be more low-key than tonight, though."

Tonight was definitely more eventful than I had expected it to be. I had planned on coming up here after my second drink to simply watch a little TV and then go to sleep. But then Shay crashed into my night, literally, and I'm so glad that she did.

"So, Jasper, who's originally from here, but not anymore, what is your biggest fear?"

"Again with the deep stuff, huh?" I gently tug a section of her hair.

I'm a loner most of the time, so having a conversation like this isn't very common for me. And it should feel odd talking to someone who is more or less a stranger while naked, but it doesn't feel weird at all. It feels refreshing.

"My biggest fear, especially after today... would be dying alone. My brother didn't have a wife or a girlfriend, just a bunch of women that he screwed around with. I don't want that to be me. But at the same time, I usually prefer to be alone in general. It's what I'm used to." I shrug my shoulders under her head. "I don't often go out, and I don't usually date."

She smiles softly at me. "You're a paradox then."

"I guess. What about you? What's your fear?"

"Well, I had intended on saying something insignificant, like getting a needle 'cause I'm terrified of them, but after hearing yours, I think I have to go a little deeper. You'll probably laugh, though."

"No, I won't."

"You probably will. It's stupid," she murmurs.

"C'mon, tell me."

She sighs. "Okay, well, I guess I fear being so boring and insignificant that people never remember who I am. You know, like, 'Who are you?' 'Uh, last night we met at such-and-such's house, and we talked for like an hour.' 'Oh, sorry, I don't remember.'"

I can't help it, I chuckle, and then she playfully hits me. "See, I told you you'd laugh."

"I'm sorry." I grab hold of the hand that's on my chest and hold it close. "I'm only laughing because you're the most memorable person I've ever met, and I simply cannot imagine anyone ever forgetting you."

"You're sweet," she says. "And I also can't imagine you as a loner, even though you were alone tonight."

"Well, it's true, although I've really enjoyed my time with you."

She pushes herself further up my body and then leans down to kiss me softly. Her lips are like heaven on mine, and I get lost in the feel of them.

Another weird sensation settles over me as I return her kiss. It's different from earlier, like this little feeling of dread. I don't like the thought of never seeing her again and never again feeling like I do right now. But I know that tonight is supposed to be left right here where it is. That's why we haven't exchanged last names, and it's why we haven't said where we're from. It's also why we won't exchange numbers, and to be completely truthful, it's most likely why I feel so comfortable with her in the first place and have acted this way.

My hands slide down her naked back, settling on her round ass as our tongues tangle together. I give her cheeks a good squeeze before I flip us so that I'm now hovering above her.

I kiss along her jaw, nibble on her earlobe, and then continue my kisses down her neck. Her hands slide over every part of my body that she can reach, causing my skin to tingle and heat. She lets out a little moan, and the feel of her underneath me and reacting to my touch like that has my dick awake and standing at attention again.

The chances of me having another condom, though, are slim to none.

"I want so badly to be inside of you again," I whisper. "But I think we're out of protection."

"Yeah, I only saw the one in your wallet. And it looked like it'd been there for a while."

"It had." I kiss her lips again while grinding my hips into her.

"Well," she breathes. "There are other things we could still do."

A wicked grin crosses my face at the thought of having a taste of her. It's another thing I haven't done in a long time. "I can think of something." I start to slide down her body, my mouth watering for a taste, but she stops me. Confused, I look back at her face and notice she's chewing on her bottom lip. "What's wrong?"

"Um, actually, do you think you could maybe...go in, just a couple of times first? I'd really like to feel you close like that. I've never done it before."

I'm pretty sure my dick just grew even bigger and harder at the thought of going bare inside her and being able to feel everything.

"Uh, are you sure that's what you want?"

She chews on her plump bottom lip some more. "Yeah, I mean, just a few times shouldn't be bad."

Oh, fuck, how badly I want to do it, even though I know we shouldn't.

So badly that I almost agree to it, but then my sensible side kicks in and deems it too risky.

"You're clean, right?" she asks when I still haven't said anything in reply.

"I am... and I really want to, so badly, but..." I trail off, letting her see the hesitation on my face.

"You're right. Of course." She shakes her head. "I don't know what I was thinking." I notice the pink on her cheeks right before she turns her head away from me as if she's embarrassed about what she offered me or something. But I don't want her feeling that way.

"Hey." I turn her chin back toward me. "Don't do that, don't feel bad."

I capture her mouth again, drowning in the pool of lust this woman surrounds me with. She's so soft and yet so forceful with her passion. She's incredible. And tonight, she's here with me.

My hands find her perky breasts, and my thumbs rub over the hard nubs, back and forth, before giving them a pinch. She gasps and squirms in response, heightening my desire for her. Wanting to devour them again, I move down her body, taking one nipple into my mouth. I swirl my tongue over it before sucking hard and moving on to the other one.

Shay's breathing starts to become erratic from just my mouth on her breasts. I can feel her chest rising and falling fast under my lips. When I glance up, I see her lips parted, tempting me for another taste.

My plan is to use my fingers while swallowing her moans in my mouth. I move up her body hastily, ready to devour her again. Only her legs are open, and she's so wet that my dick slides partway inside her. My body freezes in place, and her eyes pop open at the intrusion.

"Oh shit," I whisper, releasing a shaky breath. Because now that I'm inside her, with nothing between us, it feels way too fucking good to back out again. I've never experienced anything quite like it.

She did say earlier that she wanted me to go in just a few times. So that's what I think I'll do. Testing both her reaction and the feel of it, I move my hips back and forth a few times. Shay clings tighter to me in response, wrapping her legs around my waist. I take that as a go-ahead and push all the way in.

"Shiiiiit," I groan as my hips start rocking more with a mind of their own. "This feels incredible. I'm not sure I'll ever want to stop."

My brain actually shut down the second I slipped inside her heat. I thrust deeper inside of her, feeling everything. It's too much, it's too good, like a sensory overload. She rocks her hips at the same time I thrust, under the same spell as me, and it's taking the level of pleasure to an even higher degree.

"You feel... it feels... ohh. I think I'm coming already." And then she cries out, digging her nails into my skin. "Jasper."

Shay tries to hold me closer to her body, but I need to hold myself up so my hips can piston in and out of her faster and faster. Sweat breaks out across my body as the intensity builds. Pleasure swarms through me. This feels so fucking unreal. I can't see myself lasting much longer.

I know I need to pull out. I know it's the sensible thing to do. But god, it just feels too damn good, and my sensibilities have gone out the window.

She cries out my name again, and when I feel my balls begin to tighten and the tingling at the base of my spine, the overwhelming need to bury myself so deep inside her is so strong that it almost wins out.

Fortunately, at the last second, I manage to pull out in time to watch as streams of my cum shoot out all over her opening. It's some kind of feral, primal feeling of pride I get watching as I mark her up as if she were mine. And I know, at this moment, that I will never forget it for as long as I live.

Riley

Jasper collapses on top of me as we both come down from the amazing high that I know we *both* just experienced.

I can't believe what just happened. What I let happen. No, what I *asked* to happen. But I can't deny that I loved every second of it. I don't even know why I suggested it, really. I just had this crazy urge to be closer to him and feel every part of him.

"I'm sorry," Jasper says into my neck. "I kind of lost control for a bit."

I lift my hand and start running my fingers through his thick hair. I noticed earlier how much he enjoyed it, and he immediately leans into my hand.

"It's okay. I wanted it just as much," I say softly.

We stay lying quietly for a few minutes until his weight starts to feel a little too much for me. I can also feel the stickiness between my legs when I shift, so I'll need to take care of that right away.

He lifts himself up off of me. "Sorry, I was probably crushing you."

"A little." I smile. "I really need to get cleaned up, though."

"Oh, right, sure. Do you want to use the shower?"

"You know what? That actually sounds like a good idea." I get up and start heading toward the bathroom. But then I stop and look over my shoulder. "Care to join me?"

"I'd like that," he says with a bashful smile before following me in.

Reaching into the shower, Jasper sets the temperature before gesturing for me to get in. It's not a very small stall, but with his larger body in here with me, it makes the space seem tiny. I don't mind standing close to him, though.

My eyes drift over his tattoos once more, and I find myself tracing over the patterns again. It's not that they don't fit in with his muscular body or his dark hair and dark eyes; they absolutely do. It's just that they don't seem to fit in with his soft and kind personality.

Actually, his personality doesn't quite seem to match his looks. Maybe it's just that I've been around too many guys that are good-looking, cocky assholes, like my cheating ex, rather than the nice and quiet ones, like Jasper.

Although, after the first twenty minutes or so that we were together, he did start opening up to me more and wasn't *as* quiet.

I grab the soap from the holder and start rubbing it over his chest. "So, is there a story behind all of these?"

Jasper closes his eyes, enjoying the feel of me soaping him up. "When I was in college, it was my first time away from my parents. I wasn't particularly a part of any social group, as you can probably imagine." His eyes briefly pop open, and he gives me a small smile, but damn I find it really sexy. "Anyway, I started hanging around a couple of guys who were planning on opening a tattoo shop. I volunteered to be their guinea pig. But it was as much for me as it was for them."

"Mm, and what was *your* reason for it?" I ask as I continue running the soap over his body.

He hesitates a moment. "I didn't really grow up like most kids."

"What do you mean?" I frown.

"Well, my mother was forty-six when she had me; my father was fifty. Not quite sure what happened there." He looks at me contemplatively. "Anyway, when my school friends were off having fun, playing sports, or going to the carnival together, you know, things I wanted to do, well, I had to stay home and do chores or just read. I wasn't allowed to visit with friends very often. I didn't get to choose anything I wanted to do, actually. It only got worse in my teenage years."

I pause the hand that was soaping down his arm to consider what he just said. "That sounds really awful. I'm sorry."

He shrugs. "I accepted it back then."

Understanding dawns on me. His parents had all the control when he was younger. He wasn't *allowed* to do much, but when he got older...

"So when you got the tattoos, it was something you chose to do. You were the one with the control, and they couldn't stop you."

He gives a head nod. No wonder he's so different from the men I know. He grew up completely different from everyone I've ever known. He's unique.

I stand up on the tips of my toes, feeling the need to kiss his soft lips. His strong arms wrap around me, holding me close, and minutes tick by while we just stand together, the warm water running down our naked bodies. When he pulls back, he smiles down at me.

"You seem to be able to get a lot more information out of me than I usually give."

"Yeah?" I grin widely at him. "In that case, tell me, which one is your favorite?"

He glances down at his body and points to the one that spans from his left pec all the way up his shoulder and down to his bicep. "This one, it was my first one. One of the guys doing the tattoos was Scottish. This is a Celtic tribal design."

I run my hand over it again, unable to keep from touching him for very long. "I love it. Okay, now, what's your favorite color?"

"That's quite the subject change."

"I like asking random questions." I shrug.

Jasper tilts my chin up so that I'm facing him. "Hm, I'd say it's the color of your eyes."

I grin. "Smooth."

"It's the truth," he says genuinely. "What's yours?"

"Well, now I can't say the color of *your* eyes." I roll mine playfully.

He chuckles and takes the soap from my hand. "Nobody likes brown."

"The brown of your eyes is deep and beautiful, not just plain brown. But I think my actual favorite color is green."

He starts soaping up my body, running his hands over every inch of my skin. It's so intimate, more so than what we did earlier. It's not normal for either of us to do this sort of thing, and yet it feels completely natural, completely comfortable.

After I'm rinsed off, I grab the shampoo and squirt a little into my palm. "Turn around," I tell him.

Almost as soon as my hands touch his head and I begin to massage the shampoo into his hair, he lets out a groan and leans further into my touch. "That feels really good."

I love that he enjoys it so much. However, it does make me wonder about his childhood again. Was he shown much attention and affection throughout his life? After what he told me about his parents, it wouldn't surprise me if he wasn't.

It makes me want to shower him with touches tonight.

Tonight... *that's all we have.*

The thought has my stomach twisting. I have to keep reminding myself so that I don't get too carried away. He just makes it so easy to forget that in a few hours, we'll be nothing but memories to each other.

I gently move his head into the stream of water and run my fingers through his hair while the soap washes out. "I'm surprised you don't have women lining up to do this type of thing for you."

"Well, you'd be amazed at how quickly they move on to the next guy when you don't give them the attention and sweet talk they want."

I think about what he said for a moment. "You know, I wasn't moving on to the next guy."

"I know," he says softly. "You seemed different."

When all the soap is gone, I wrap my arms around his waist and rest my cheek on his back.

"Do you want me to wash your hair?" Jasper asks.

"No, that's okay. I actually washed it this morning. I just want to stay like this for a second."

He threads his fingers through mine across his stomach, and once again, we stand quietly under the warm spray of the shower.

CHAPTER THREE

Jasper

I grab the two folded towels that are on the rack, and wrap one around her body before drying myself off with the other one and wrapping it around my hips.

It's already around one o'clock in the morning, but I'm not ready for this night to end yet.

"Are you hungry?" I ask. "This hotel has twenty-four-hour room service, so we can have something brought up if you like."

She glances up at me from drying her legs. "That sounds great. I was just thinking about how I'd love a bowl of strawberries."

"I'll see what they have," I murmur, prying my eyes off her legs again.

Heading out of the bathroom, I search for the menu I saw

earlier. I'm glad she agreed to get something to eat and stay longer. For a second there, I thought she'd say no and leave. For the last few minutes in the shower, she was quieter than she had been earlier and just stood there hugging me. Not that I'm complaining about that part, it felt good to be hugged by her. To be touched by her.

But it almost seemed like she was getting ready to say goodbye.

I find the menu and then order a few different items for the both of us to share. She's still in the bathroom, so I pull back the covers on the bed and turn the TV on before sliding in. I'm just getting comfortable when she finally comes out looking distracted.

"Everything okay?" I ask.

She gives me a soft smile while climbing onto the bed beside me. "Yes, everything is good."

"I ordered a fruit salad 'cause they don't have bowls of only strawberries. She said it has a lot of strawberries in it, though. I also got a chicken dish and some fries."

"Sounds perfect."

She snuggles against my side, and I lean into her touch, pulling her close. How is it that I only met this woman mere hours ago? She makes me feel a type of familiarity and comfort you get from knowing someone a lot longer.

"So, Jasper, what do you do in your spare time?"

I notice that she didn't ask me what I do for work. It's another reminder to me that this ends here, tonight, and she doesn't *need* to know what I do for a living. At least, that's how I see it. But what I do in my spare time, that, she *wants* to know.

"I read a lot."

"Just like when you were a kid?" she asks, trailing her fingers over my bare stomach.

"Yes."

"Do you read at home alone? Or do you go somewhere to read?"

I start rubbing a hand up and down her arm, feeling her soft skin under my fingertips. "I read at home."

"Hmm, well, there's this beautiful place where I live that I've been to a bunch of times." She angles her head to look up at me. "It has books that you can read there, or you can bring your own. Kind of like a library, but not. There are a couple of fireplaces and some plants. The couches are comfy. It's so peaceful, it makes you feel like you're not alone, and yet, you can quietly read on your own."

"That sounds nice. I think there is a place similar to that where I'm from."

"You should check it out," she urges.

"I might."

"Something tells me that you won't."

I smile down at her. "I might."

A few minutes later, our food arrives, and we end up eating in companionable silence while a murder mystery show plays on the TV. I'm all too aware that every minute that passes is a minute closer to her leaving this room, a minute closer to her leaving my life.

Every second becomes more precious than the last.

After finishing our food, she turns to me while we're still leaning against the headboard of the bed. "So, I know that you had a brother. Do you have any other siblings?"

"No."

She laughs softly when I don't say anything more, like I was supposed to elaborate or something. "Always a man of many words."

"Sorry."

"Don't apologize. I'm just teasing."

I give the silky strands of her hair that I'm playing with a little tug. "Do you have any siblings?"

"I have an older sister." She sighs. "She's the better of us two."

Frowning, I ask, "What do you mean?"

Shay slides down so that she's lying on her back, and I move down beside her. "Well, she owns a business, so she's successful. I just work for her sometimes. She's also married and has a daughter, so she has her life put together. The last relationship I had was with a cheater. Plus, I've always thought she was prettier." She laughs at that last part.

I tilt her chin to look toward me. "Well, I know that that can't be true because you're the most amazing and most beautiful woman I've ever met."

Her eyes soften as she looks up at me and places a hand on my cheek.

"Thank you," she whispers.

I take hold of her hand, turning my face to kiss her palm before leaning down to kiss her lips. Every touch of skin and every stroke of tongue, has me becoming more addicted to her. I don't try to do anything more than taste her lips, though. This is enough. Her kissing me back, tangling her fingers through my hair while I lean over her, kissing her deeply, is enough.

Exhaustion begins to take hold of both of us as the night continues on. So, I bring her in close to me, pull the blanket up over us, and close my eyes.

"You won't be here when I wake up, will you." It's a statement, not a question. I know.

Her eyes are closed as well, but her fingers are tracing over my chest and arms. "Probably not," she whispers.

I try to ignore the knot that forms in my gut. Tonight, that's all we had. That's all we planned for. With that thought, I hold her tighter and kiss the top of her head.

"Well, I hope I don't wake up for a very long time."

CHAPTER FOUR

Jasper - Five months later

"Would you like to know the sex?" I ask the couple in front of me.

They face each other and share a smile. "Yes," the husband says when he turns back to me.

I nod and face the screen again, moving the transducer around to find the right area. When I find it, there's no doubt about what I see.

"Congratulations. You're having a boy."

"A boy," the woman says to her husband.

"I love you," he replies, leaning over to kiss her.

I finish up with all the necessary information I need to gather and leave them alone for a moment while I check in with the doctor to make sure he's happy with the images I got. I've studied enough to know that they *are* good enough, but it's standard procedure.

Once I return, I give one of the better pictures of the baby to the couple, and we say our goodbyes. It's lunchtime after they leave, so I get my lunch out of the fridge in the break room and take a seat to eat.

"Hey, JD," Tia says. She's one of the other Sonographers here. JD is what they started calling me shortly after I started here since my last name is DeLarouge.

"Hi." I nod my head once at her.

She sits down at the same table as me but pulls her phone out, knowing that we won't be having much of a conversation.

I have tried. When I came back from my trip to Fairfield, I did try. I tried to replicate those same feelings I had that night with Shay. I've tried to form friendships beyond just knowing my colleague's names'.

I *liked* talking to Shay about things.

I *liked* being close to her.

So when I had awoken to an empty bed that morning, *I* felt empty too.

However much I've tried, though, I've still never felt the same as I did when I was with Shay. And you can't change your personality after just one night, so while I've made some effort to talk to others and have improved a little on the small talk, as well as made friends with Patrick, the ophthalmologist upstairs, I'm still the same quiet guy I was before.

"Hi, JD," Maya, one of the receptionists, stands next to the table I'm at, smiling down at me.

"Hi," I reply.

Unlike Tia, Maya hovers there in the same spot for several

moments, like she wants to say something more or is waiting for me to ask her to join me before finally moving on.

My day continues on with "hellos" to people as we pass by each other in the hallways and more reciting the standard instructions or questions for the patients that I see. It's mostly quiet, with little interaction.

At the end of the day, when I'm reaching for the door handle of my vehicle, Patrick saunters up to me and leans against the hood of my car.

"JD, what you up to tonight?"

"Not much," I say as I deposit my bag into the passenger side.

He crosses his arms. "You should come for a beer with a couple of my buddies and me."

"Ah, no thanks."

"How did I know you were going to say that?" He chuckles. "One day, I'll get you to come. Hey, maybe you can come to poker night in a few weeks."

"Maybe," I answer.

"Alright, well, I'll catch ya later, then." He pushes off my car and pats my shoulder as he passes me by.

"See ya."

I sit down in the driver's seat and watch as he gets in his own car and drives off. I like Patrick. He accepts me as I am and doesn't seem to care when I decline his offer to do something and don't talk much. He generally talks enough for three people anyway.

I pull out of the parking lot and head towards my usual Friday night place to hang out. I've been going to The Reading Nook almost every Friday evening since Shay and I talked about it. Well, she had told me about the place where she lived, and it reminded me of this place.

She was right about how you feel like you're not alone, and yet, I never get interrupted while I read. A few women look at me like they want to talk, but when I don't go out of my way to say anything to them, they go back to their reading again.

Once I arrive, I find my preferred spot by the fireplace and get comfortable. I take a quick glance at my surroundings before pulling out my book and a bottle of water. Briefly, I wonder if Shay has been to the place she told me about that's similar to here. Then, I open my book and begin reading.

A couple of hours later, my stomach grumbles, reminding me that I need to have some dinner. Closing my book, I stretch out my neck and then stand to stretch out my legs and shoulders.

I'm just packing my stuff away when my gaze drifts across the large room and the people that are sitting there reading quietly. But my eyes stop dead in their tracks when they land on a woman sitting over by the windows, looking in my direction. The water bottle drops out of my hand and rolls under the chair I was sitting in.

"Shay," I whisper.

She's here.

What is she doing here, in my city?

I shake my head at myself. *She's here.* So what does it matter *why* she is?

My heart rate increases as excitement stirs in my blood. A smile forms on my face. My biggest regret from that night was not getting her phone number so that we could have at least kept in contact and talked again.

My feet start leading me in the direction of where she's sitting. She's staring blankly across the room, but when her eyes do land on me, her lack of reaction has me pausing in my tracks.

Does she not remember me?

What if our night together meant nothing to her, and she hasn't even thought about it once?

I've thought about her and our night together every single day.

I stand there staring at her while she looks at me without even a flicker of recognition on her face, and then she turns her head slightly away. She has no idea who I am. I'm an idiot to think that I would have been on her mind at all.

I'm still standing here, frozen in place, when another woman passes me by. "Excuse me," she says, looking at me with a raised eyebrow.

That's when I realize I'm half blocking the walkway leading into the section where Shay is sitting. I watch, still unmoving, while the woman walks toward Shay.

"Riley, why did you ask me to meet you here?" The woman that walked past me leans down and kisses Shay's cheek.

Wait a second, what?

She said *Riley*.

That's not Shay? But she looks exactly the same as her. The same dark hair, same face, and from here, she appears to have the same color eyes, even though they do lack the same sparkle I saw in them that night.

I guess the fact that she's *not* Shay would explain why she didn't recognize me, though.

My body deflates. It isn't her.

Even with that knowledge, I don't move from the spot. I still can't seem to look away from them, and I can't seem to force my feet to leave.

"I just felt the need to be here," the woman named Riley answers.

Even her voice sounds the same. But maybe it's just my memory tricking me, finding similarities and telling me that it's the same because the resemblance is incredible.

"Come on, let's go to dinner." The other woman reaches down and grabs *Riley's* hand to help her up.

I don't understand why she needs any help until she's standing and I see her stomach, her *pregnant* stomach. The weirdest sensation travels through my body, and I think about Shay being pregnant with my child.

But this isn't Shay. This is a woman named Riley. And yet, I still can't seem to take my eyes off her. It's not until they begin walking toward me that I'm snapped out of whatever trance I was in.

The final confirmation is given that she indeed is not my Shay when I notice that this woman is using a white cane to feel the ground in front of her, like people who are blind or visually impaired do. Shay definitely wasn't blind.

I watch as they get closer to me, still unable to turn around and leave for some reason. Only when the other woman frowns at me do I step aside to let them through. I'm sure she's wondering what I'm doing still standing here, just as much as I am.

When they start to pass me, the woman called Riley turns her head as if she's looking up at me. All the air gets sucked out of my lungs when I see her face this close. I can't believe how much she looks like Shay.

But her name is *Riley*, not Shay. I keep reminding myself.

Riley looks at me for a few seconds. At least, it *feels* like she's looking at me. I'm not sure what she sees or if she can see anything at all. And being this close, I can now see the cloudiness in her eyes.

They continue walking, and I watch as they make their way to the exit, the other woman guiding Riley the whole way. At the last second, Riley looks over her shoulder in my direction. But there is no smile like Shay had given me that night. It's just a blank stare in my general area.

A second later, they're gone, and I'm left standing here with the weirdest feeling swarming in my gut. I force myself back to the chair where my bag still sits and lower myself into it. I can't explain these feelings I'm having or the reaction that I had to that woman. It has to simply be that she looked so similar to Shay.

I shake my head and reach under the chair to locate my water bottle. All the hunger pains I had earlier have vanished since the weird encounter, so on the way home, instead of grabbing some takeout as I had planned, I head towards the grocery store instead.

I'm suddenly feeling like a bowl of strawberries.

CHAPTER FIVE

Riley

I laugh at the shock in my sister's voice through the speakerphone in my car. "I'm sorry I didn't tell you earlier. I just needed to get my head wrapped around it before I said anything to you."

"And you're sure?"

"Yes, I'm sure! Three pregnancy tests can't be wrong."

"Okay, that's true." She sighs. "And you're sure it's this Jasper guy that you told me about?"

"Yes, and I'm a little insulted that you'd think I wouldn't know who the father is. I haven't been with anyone else since that loser, Pax, who cheated on me."

"I'm sorry, Riley-bear. You know I didn't mean it like that. Do you have any way of contacting him?"

I sigh this time while clicking the indicator on and turning the corner. "I emailed him, but I never heard anything back. Well, I'm not even sure it was his email address, to be honest. I just saw the little piece of paper in his wallet and took it."

"It didn't have his name on it, I'm guessing?"

"All that was on it was JTD40379@hotmail.com. I figured it could have been his initials."

She laughs. "Who carries around their own email address?"

"I *do*," I answer, irritated. "When I make a new one and don't remember it."

"I'm sorry. Well, you know I'll be here for–"

The sound of screeching tires and crunching metal pierces through my ears before pain shoots through my head and body, and then everything goes black.

I wake up with a start, clutching at my chest and breathing heavily. It's the same dream I have had at least once every couple of weeks ever since it happened. My hand slides down to my belly, and I rub circles over it until I've calmed myself down.

My shirt is soaked through, and my hair is damp with sweat. I stand up, feeling my way to the chair in the corner of my room. It's where I keep an extra nightshirt for times like these when I need to change. With a nice clean and dry shirt on, I pull the hair tie off my wrist and twist my hair up into a messy bun. Then I slide my hand along the wall as I make my way into the kitchen for some water.

I can see the light from the fridge break through the darkness in front of me, but I see nothing else, definitely not the contents. I grope at the items in the door until I find the handle of the jug I'm looking for. Once I've located a cup as well, I bring the cup and the jug over to the sink and try carefully pouring some water into the cup. I'm successful this time and smile at the small victory.

Making my way into the living room, I have Alexa turn the lights on so that I can make out the shadow of my couch.

After the accident, my sister begged me to come live with her and her family, but after adamantly refusing, she helped set up my apartment so that I would be able to live in it alone.

We got rid of a lot of the clutter, along with any unnecessary things that could be potentially hazardous to me. We also replaced anything light that I had with darker items.

She was the one who set up Alexa for me and made sure I could access everything through her... well, *it*.

As I settle on my couch, I rub my belly again. I've felt unsettled for most of the afternoon, and I had this strong urge to go to that book place earlier today. And, well, since I like to follow my gut, I went.

For the first month after meeting Jasper, I went there often. It was sort of a way to feel close to him, and I often wondered if he ever went to the place that he had told me about that was similar.

I stopped going after my accident, though. What good is a place for reading books when you can't even see them?

Regardless of that fact, I followed my instincts today and went to The Reading Nook. I'm not sure how long I sat, staring straight ahead, but then I saw that dark shadow approach. The person was still far enough away that I couldn't tell which way they were facing, but something told me that they were facing me. And by the size of the shadow, I knew it was a man. I've had time to learn these things over the past few months.

I'm not sure what it was that I felt by his presence. It definitely wasn't fear, but it was *something*.

It wasn't until my sister and I were passing by him that I felt something so familiar that I just had to look up at the shadowy figure. I could just tell that he was looking at me too. But I had to resign myself to the fact that if he knew me, he would have said something to me.

My mind flicks back to Jasper. I've thought about him so much since that night. He deserves to know about the baby, *his* baby. I just wish I knew where he lived or how to get in contact with him other than the random email address I took.

Before I snuck out of his hotel room early that morning, I had kissed his soft lips, traced my fingers over his chest one more time, and then got dressed. I was almost out the door when I saw his wallet out of the corner of my eye. I looked back at the beautiful man sleeping peacefully on the bed and then picked it up. I had stared at it for a few moments, contemplating, before opening it.

I wanted so badly to look at his license and find out his full name and where he lived, but I didn't want to torture myself with finding out something like the fact that he lived on the other side of the country. Stupid, I know. It didn't occur to me until it was too late that I could have possibly found out the opposite as well, that he lived close to me.

I had remembered the little piece of paper with an email address on it that I saw when I got the condom out earlier and made the rash decision to take it before leaving his hotel room. It was a long shot to hope it was his. Not many people have their own email addresses written down in their wallets. But it still felt better to at least have it. At least, it did, until I got no reply back.

"Alexa, do I have any emails from JTD40379@hotmail.com?"

When she tells me that I don't, I sigh and smile down at my stomach. "I didn't think so."

It's been a while since I had last checked, and even though I knew what the answer would be, I wanted to hear it anyway.

"Alexa, can you send a message to Jordan at nine A.M tomorrow morning?"

"What is the message for Jordan?"

"Hey, beautiful, happy six-year anniversary! I hope you and Troy have a great day. Love you."

"Your message to Jordan is scheduled to be sent at nine A.M tomorrow morning."

Jordan will probably shake her head and then call me as soon as she gets it. I literally just had dinner with her tonight and gave her a card that I had Mia write out for me. That reminds me, I should call Mia tomorrow as well.

As I lean my head back on the couch, I feel the flutter of the baby kicking. It fills me with pure joy.

The only kind of joy I've felt lately.

My life has become a series of voice commands and a daily struggle to remain independent. A far cry from what it used to be.

"Alexa, what time is my appointment on Monday?"

"You have an appointment at *Your Health Imaging* at eleven forty-five A.M."

I always love getting the chance to hear my baby's heartbeat, and it's something I will look forward to all weekend.

I let out a loud yawn. "Alexa, what time is it?"

"The time is eleven fifty-seven P.M."

No wonder I still feel really tired. I was barely asleep for two hours. I lay down on the couch and pull the throw blanket over my body, too lazy to go back to my bed.

"Alexa, turn off the lights."

All the varying shades of gray and black that I see disappear, and I'm left in complete darkness. But sweet thoughts of Jasper fill my mind as I drift off to sleep.

CHAPTER SIX

Jasper

I know my next appointment is here, and yet, I hesitate to call her in.

When I saw the name Riley Brooks on the chart, I knew it wasn't necessarily the same Riley I saw on Friday night. It's not like she's the only person to ever have that name. But it had made me pause nonetheless. Then, sure enough, when I peeked around the corner of the waiting room, there she sat. The woman I saw at The Reading Nook. The same woman that was stuck on my mind all weekend.

Well, to be honest, my mind would flit between her and Shay over and over. I couldn't tell if it was because of the way *she* made me feel or if it was simply because she looked so much like Shay.

"Everything okay, JD?" Tia asks as she passes me.

"Yes."

Raising a single eyebrow at me, she continues on. I take a deep breath and finally step into the waiting room after five minutes of standing here, watching her.

"Riley Brooks," I call out, looking directly at her.

"That's me." She lifts the bag on her lap and shuffles to the edge of her seat before standing. Then, she feels for her cane leaning against the chair beside her.

I move toward her and offer an arm. "Here, I can lead you."

"Thank you." She smiles in the direction of my face but doesn't lock eyes with me.

Just the gentle feel of her delicate fingers on my skin gives me a small rush that comes from being touched and getting affection. I'm sure it's simply from the lack of it shown to me while growing up and not particularly because it's from her.

With Riley's hand on my arm, I lead her to the little room we'll be using for her appointment. The whole time, my heart continues to race, and I'm not too sure why. It's got to be simply the fact that she looks like Shay.

I get her situated on the bed and take a seat. "I'll need you to lift your shirt for me, please."

She does as I ask, and I cover her lower half with a special sheet, tucking it into her waistband.

"Is anyone joining you today?" I ask. For all I know, she's married or has a boyfriend.

"No, it's just me. My sister and a couple of my friends said they wanted to come, but I guess the stubborn side of me insisted on doing it alone since I'll be doing the whole pregnancy alone." I frown at her comment, and then, as if she can see my reaction, she adds, "The father isn't in the picture, but it's okay."

I'm not sure why she told me that. It's none of my business, really. But I still take hold of that piece of information and tuck it away like it's treasure.

I notice she seems a little tense, and for some reason, I don't want her feeling that way, so I touch her arm just briefly. "I'm sure you'll do great on your own."

Her shoulders seem to drop an inch as they relax, and her head lulls to the side so that she's now facing me. "Thank you. You have a nice voice, by the way. It's very soothing."

"Thanks." I smile.

"I haven't heard of any males doing ultrasounds before," she says. "Sorry, I guess that may sound rude."

I get the gel out and prepare to start. "No, it's fine. It's true that there are a lot more women in this industry, but there are other men out there who are Sonographers as well. More so in other fields. I started out doing vascular."

"Do you enjoy it?"

"I do." I realize I've talked more with her than I usually do with any other patients. It must be because she's alone. "I'm going to put some gel onto your stomach now and take a look. Don't worry. It's warm."

"Okay." She smiles at me, and I'm a little confused by the effect it's having on me.

I clear my throat and turn my attention to the screen to do my job, taking measurements, getting images, and just generally checking things over. I've studied enough to know what I'm looking at, and I know that everything is looking good and appears to be on track for around twenty weeks. The briefest thought that it has been around that long since I've seen Shay crosses my mind. But I shake my head and continue on.

After a few minutes, I glance over at her and watch as she stares up at the ceiling. I can't imagine what it would be like to be blind. I wonder if she's ever been able to see? Or was she born blind?

I'm startled out of my thoughts when she turns her head toward me and speaks, "Everything okay?"

"Yes."

"I just noticed that you stopped moving, and I couldn't hear the clicking of your computer."

"Oh, no, everything is fine." I shift on my chair. "Did you want to find out the sex?"

She hums and then places her hand on her stomach, probably out of habit. "Oh, whoops," she says. "I forgot about the gel."

"Here, let me." I lift her hand and gently wipe it clean. An assortment of weird feelings run through me at the touch of her soft hand.

"Thank you," she says softly.

"So, the sex?" I ask, sitting back again.

"I think I'll wait. It's not like I can pick colored stuff out for him or her anyway."

"No, but your friends and family could."

"That's true... I still think I'll wait."

"Okay." I move the transducer around a little more, stare at the baby on the screen, and swallow past the lump in my throat.

Having a reaction to Riley, I can somewhat understand. She reminds me in almost every way of the woman who made an impact on my life. But having a reaction to her baby? Well, that just doesn't make sense.

I stand up abruptly. "I'm just going to check with the doctor and make sure he has all the images he needs. I'll be right back."

"Okay." She smiles again.

Walking faster than I normally do, I make my way to the doctor to check in with him. Then I make it back in record time. I just didn't want her to be alone for too long.

"Are you doing okay?" I ask, retaking my seat.

"Yes, thank you."

Another couple of minutes go by. "Well, I've gotten everything I need to get here, so we're all finished."

"Oh, um, is it possible to hear the heartbeat before I leave? The last time I had an ultrasound done, they did that."

"Of course." I don't know why I didn't do that already. Too distracted, I guess.

I turn the sound on and find the right spot to be able to hear it best. The pure happiness on her face does things to me. A thought crosses my mind. Usually, we'd give a picture of the baby to take home, but that won't be any good for her.

"Do you want to record the heartbeat?" I ask her.

Her face brightens even more. "I would love that." She frowns. "But how?"

"Do you have your phone?"

"Yeah," she says, her face brightening again. "It's in the outside pocket of my bag."

"Are you okay with me getting it?" I ask.

"Yes. Thank you."

I go and retrieve her phone and bring it back to her. "Here you go."

"Do you mind doing it for me?" She presses her thumb on the screen to unlock it and then turns it toward me.

"Okay."

I take the phone from her and notice that her home screen is a picture of her with a group of girls at the beach. All of them are wearing sunglasses and smiling while lying on towels. I'm struck with another sense of familiarity, but I quickly shake my head and find the recording app. I can't keep comparing her to another woman.

Once I've got the recording for her, I help her get cleaned up and then stand.

After stepping out of the room, she turns to me. "Do you mind guiding me to the restroom?"

"Of course." I lead her across the hallway and then stand outside the door, waiting for her. Most women need to stop in here right after they're finished with their appointment, but I never usually wait for them.

"Thank you," Riley says after coming out. I offer her my arm again, and we start walking down the hall toward the front reception. "Oh, I didn't even get your name."

Just as she mentions that, Cristina, one of the other Sonographers, approaches. "JD, Doctor Irlum, would like to talk to us after lunch. He asked me to let you know."

"Sure," I tell her, and then she takes off as quickly as she arrived, with a short head nod.

"Well, I guess that answers that. Nice to meet you, JD," Riley says, giving my arm a squeeze.

We reach the end of the hall, and this is where I should say goodbye. This is where I should turn around and go eat my lunch... But Shay's words spring forth in my mind.

"So, I have this thing. That when you feel a certain spark or connection with someone, you should see what it's about. You should at least talk to the person."

"See you, JD," Riley says.

When she turns around to leave, that same feeling of panic from the thought of never seeing her again rushes at me, and I reach out for her arm.

"Riley." Pausing, she turns around. I grab at the back of my neck, squeezing the muscles. I don't know what I'm doing. "It's my lunch." She tilts her head to the side, waiting for me to elaborate. "Would you like to grab something to eat at the cafe across the street with me?"

Her head dips down to face the ground as she considers. I know it's weird for me to be asking a pregnant stranger to eat with me. But when have I ever fit in with the 'norm'?

Looking back up at me, she smiles sweetly. "Sure, that would be nice."

CHAPTER SEVEN

Riley

Following my gut has never led me astray. Sure, it hasn't always resulted in something great, but it's never led me to something bad.

I don't see ending up pregnant after one night with Jasper as being bad because that night was incredible, and that man was beautiful. It's a night that I will never forget, and not just because of the obvious reason of a baby resulting from it. A baby who has kept me from becoming too depressed about losing my sight as well. I'm excited to meet him or her and hold them in my arms. I'm happy to know that I've kept a piece of Jasper with me.

My gut is also the reason I agreed to have lunch with JD. There is something so familiar and calming about him.

Is it weird to ask a pregnant, blind woman, who you just

did an ultrasound on, to lunch? Maybe. But maybe he just wants company? Maybe he's just lonely? I could hear a kind of loneliness and yearning in his voice. I think now that I can't see facial expressions, I've learned to pick up on the tones in people's voices.

JD leads me across the street, and the whole time, he has his hand placed over mine on his arm. It feels nice. I'm familiar with the cafe we're going to from when I still had my sight. In fact, the woman who owns it knows my sister well.

She's very nice, but if I'm really lucky, she won't be here today, and therefore can't tell my sister. I can only imagine what she'd have to say.

"Here," JD says once we're inside and he's found us a table.

I sit down and place my bag at my feet so that I know where it is at all times.

"Riley! Look at you," Sheryl, the owner says. "I haven't seen you in so long!" Her voice gets louder as she gets closer to us. I guess I'm not so lucky today, but maybe just maybe, she won't say anything to Jordan.

"Hi, Sheryl," I answer.

"Look at your belly. It's so cute! Do you know what you're having yet?"

"No, I decided not to find out."

"Oh, well, that'll be a nice surprise," she pauses, "And who's this?"

I know she's talking about the man sitting across from me. "This is JD."

"Hello," JD says politely.

"Nice to meet you," she coos. "Now, can I get you guys a drink to start off with?"

"I'll just have water please," I say, leaning back in my chair.

"Sure thing, and for you?" she asks JD.

"Coffee, please."

"Coming right up," Sheryl tells us.

I see her shadow move away and then turn back to the figure across the table from me.

"Have you eaten here before?" I ask.

"Just once. I usually bring my lunch from home."

"That's good. It certainly saves money not buying food every day." I smile in his direction. "Do you cook?"

"I do," he says. "I make a few dishes on Sunday to eat throughout the week."

"Smart. My sister usually makes some containers for me so that all I have to do is heat them up."

"That's nice of her." I watch his shadowy figure move, and I imagine his elbows leaning on the table with his chin propped on his knuckles.

"It is. I probably wouldn't eat very well otherwise. You can't exactly cook when you're blind, and you never know what you're putting into the dish or your mouth." I attempt to make a joke, but it falls flat. I'm about to apologize when I see another shadow approach us, along with the scent of perfume.

"There you are, JD. When I didn't see you in the lunchroom, I wondered where you might be."

Remember that yearning I was talking about earlier? Yeah, this woman has it, only it's the other type of yearning. The type of yearning with the sexual undertone. She wants him. And suddenly, I realize why he must have asked me here in the first place.

"I'm eating lunch here today," JD answers her.

"Okay . . . well, um. I guess I'll see you back at the clinic after."

"Sure. Bye, Maya."

Embarrassment and anger start to bubble up from within me. It's not often that I feel this way, and I'm usually a pretty easygoing person.

I've taken the blame when Jordan did something wrong, and I didn't want her to get in trouble with our mother when we were younger. When I had my sight in the past, I made myself the reason for a mistake made at the restaurant so that the other girls wouldn't get into trouble. I don't mind covering for people. But for some reason, being this guy's convenient pathetic excuse so that he doesn't have to face something uncomfortable really irks me.

I wait until I see her shadow move away from us – I'm not a bitch after all – and then I stand up from my seat. "You know, this is pretty low of you."

"What?"

"What happened? You guys hook up, and now she won't leave you alone?" I speak low enough that only he can hear me. "You didn't want an awkward encounter in the lunchroom, so you thought, 'here's a pathetic lonely, pregnant, blind woman, what a perfect excuse to get me out of it?'"

He stands up abruptly, his chair scraping along the ground. "No! That's not... I never–"

"Thanks, but I think I'll be going now."

I turn to leave, but right away, I feel his hand on my arm, gentle, not forceful. "Wait, *please*."

It's the sound of that 'please' that has me stopping. It reminds me of Jasper when I first went to step away from him that night. Slightly desperate and a little vulnerable. He somehow doesn't sound like a guy that's just using me as an excuse. I gave Jasper a chance after assuming he didn't want to talk to me, and it led me to something incredible. A connection I've never had before. This guy deserves at least a chance to talk as well, so I turn to face him and wait to hear what he has to say.

"I've never been with her, not even close. I just... I just wanted your company, I swear. Please stay."

My heart melts a little at his words. Every bit of reservation and anger I had, seems to leave my body at once, and I nod slowly. "Okay."

I hear him let out a breath. "Thank you." We retake our seats, and he says, "I'm sorry for making you feel that way."

This guy.

"No." I place my hand on the table in front of me and blow out a heavy breath. "Don't be sorry. I'm the one who should apologize. I've just become more sensitive, I guess, since becoming blind." I kind of feel bad for what I accused him of now, but I can't take it back. I'll just try to be nicer from here on.

"It's okay, I get it," he says, and then after a minute, adds, "So, you weren't always blind?"

"No, and I'm not completely blind either. I can usually make out darker figures, like you right now, and anything dark against a light background. All my furniture is dark."

"Do you live alone?" he asks. "I mean because you mentioned that your sister brings you food."

"Yeah, I do. I've tried to keep things normal." I shake my head. "Well, as normal as they can be."

I'm surprised when I feel his hand land on top of mine on the table. It feels warm and strong. "I think you're admirable."

"Thank you," I say quietly, feeling emotions clog my throat.

A beat passes where he's simply holding my hand on top

of the table.

"Okay, guys, sorry about the delay. I just had to take care of a phone call out back." I slide my hand out from under his and sit up straighter. "Here's your water and your coffee. Now, do you know what you want to eat?" Sheryl asks.

"Do you still have the special cheese melt with bacon and tomato in it?"

"You bet we do, my dear. Would you like one?"

Smiling, I answer, "Yes, please."

"Okay, and for you?" she asks JD.

"I'll have the same."

When she leaves the table, I reach out to feel for my glass of water but then feel both of his hands enclose mine. A tingle sparks at the point of contact and travels up my arm, causing my breath to hitch. I'm not sure if he notices it at all. He guides my hand to wrap around the glass and then holds them there a beat longer than necessary.

"Thank you," I say softly.

He doesn't say anything for a long while after taking his hands off mine. The sounds of the chatter around us and the clanking of cutlery on plates fill the silence between us.

"I'm glad you asked me here for lunch," I finally say.

"Yeah?"

"Yes," I answer. "I like acting on instincts and taking chances."

He's quiet for another moment and then asks, "Do you have a twin?"

"What?" I laugh at his random question. "No, no twin."

"Were you adopted?"

I chuckle again. What weird questions. "No, not adopted either. Why?"

"Sorry, it's just that you remind me of someone."

"Oh?" I raise an eyebrow. "In a good way, I hope."

"Yes."

I guess that could have contributed to his decision to ask me to join him here for lunch. I'm not quite sure how I feel about that. But then again, he also reminds me of Jasper, the way he's nice and gentle and doesn't talk a whole lot. And I have to admit, that has me feeling even better about being here and probably contributed to me saying yes.

We fall into silence again, but it's comfortable. I just wish I knew what he was looking at because I've been looking at his dark gray shadow most of the time.

Our lunch arrives, and we spend the rest of the time asking a few questions about generic things back and forth while we eat. I do most of the talking, but I don't mind.

When it's time for JD to return to work, we say our goodbyes, but I can tell that he's watching and waiting for me to get into the cab he waved down for me, and the fact that he seems to care sends a warm rush through my insides.

On the drive home, I try to sort out what these odd feelings are that I'm getting toward him, a person who's virtually a stranger, but then my sister's ringtone cuts through my thoughts and draws my attention to my phone. I have a feeling I know exactly what this will be about, and since I'm not particularly in the mood to share my personal life with the cab driver, I let it go to voicemail. A second later, I get a text which is also from her. That, too, I will wait to listen to until I'm home.

A few minutes later, we pull up to the curb. The cab driver offers his help, but I decline. Using my cane, I feel around until I hit the unmistakable edges of the giant pot of flowers with the round base and the cracked and crumbling concrete right beneath it. That tells me that I'm outside the right building and that the door is four steps away.

Inside my apartment, I play the voicemail first. *"Hey, Riley-bear. I just heard from Sheryl, and she told me you were in her cafe with a really handsome guy. Who was he? I thought you had an appointment?"*

I roll my eyes. Yep, I knew it. Next, I get Alexa to read my text message. *"Just tried calling you, hope everything is okay. Who are you with?"*

Deciding to stop her from freaking out, I call her up.

"Thank goodness," she says when she answers. "I was worried."

"Will you stop babying me? I'm fine."

She sighs. "You know I get worried when you're out and about, and you didn't text me after your appointment."

That's right, I forgot. "Sorry, I went for lunch right afterward."

"Yeah, Sheryl told me you were there...so who was the guy? Sheryl said he was really good-looking."

Good-looking, huh? Well, I wouldn't know about that.

I contemplate what I should tell her. I love her, but she has been way too overprotective of me since the accident. I can't really blame her, though. Our dad left when we were little, with the promise to still spend time with us girls and have us come stay with him, but that never happened. He just...forgot about us. Then our mother died when we were teenagers, so we only had each other for a long time.

"His name is JD."

"Okaaaay, and he's a friend of yours? Sheryl said it looked like you guys were pretty friendly and that he barely took his eyes off you."

Sheryl seems to have a lot of things to say about me after a simple lunch.

But what she said about JD staring at me has that same warm feeling from earlier returning. I'm not really sure how to feel about that, so I brush off her comment. "Well, I don't know about that. He just wanted company."

"What do you mean?"

I settle into the couch behind me. "He . . . he did my ultrasound, and then it was his lunch break."

"What? Why–"

"Don't." I cut her off. "He just wanted to eat some lunch."

She's silent for a moment but then can't hold back. "I don't like the sounds of that, Riley. It sounds creepy. Who does that?" she asks. "Is he some creeper that just prays on unsuspecting pregnant women that he performs ultrasounds on? That's just weird."

"Yes, because no one would ever want to have lunch with a single, pregnant woman, right?" I feel myself getting worked up, and the tears are starting to form already.

"Riley–"

"Oh, and don't forget blind!" I say, sitting up straighter. "No one would want my company, right?"

"Stop it, Riley!"

"Look, I get it, okay. Guys wouldn't exactly jump at the chance to spend time with me. And yes, it is a little odd, but I never got the feeling of anything malicious from him, Jordan." I shrug. "He just seemed lonely, okay?"

She's silent for another moment before she sighs. "I'm sorry. I just . . . you're right. I need to trust you more. You've always had good instincts. You're a grown woman, and you can hang out with whoever you want to."

"Yes, I can. Thank you."

"You're a gorgeous woman. I'm not surprised a handsome ultrasound technician wants to hang out with you. There are probably other men that would like to as well."

I snort. "Alright, alright. No need to lay it on so thick. Anyway, it was just lunch, and then we went our separate ways, okay? We didn't exchange numbers or anything." Although, he did hesitate at the end, just as much as I did. But really, why would he want my number anyway? I need to be realistic. What I said before is not entirely inaccurate. "Listen, Jordan. I'm tired, so I'm going to take a nap now."

"Wait! Did you find out what the sex of the baby is?"

"No, I decided to wait."

"Oh, okay. Well, since you missed today, if you feel like coming into the restaurant tomorrow to work the front for a few hours, you know you're welcome."

"Thanks, I probably will."

Ever since the accident, my work options have been severely limited. I was supposed to go to school for nursing this year and just work part-time for my sister until I got a job in that field, but those plans had to change, obviously. Now, most days, I simply greet people at my sister's restaurant and answer the phone for her. My four-year-old niece, Sasha, goes there after daycare, so I hang out with her as well.

"Okay, see you tomorrow, Riley-bear. Love you."

"Love you too, bye."

I get up and manage to pour myself some milk with minimal spillage, then I make my way to my bedroom, collapsing onto the bed to take a nap.

This time, it's a mixture of thoughts between JD and Jasper that fill my mind as I close my eyes and drift off to sleep.

CHAPTER EIGHT

Jasper

After getting back to work, I go and meet with the doctor right away. We start discussing the possibility of switching to a new program, and Cristina and I let him know our thoughts. Well, Cristina mostly tells him, but I do mention a thing or two. In the end, we all agree to give it a trial run.

"I think we should get the patients that had appointments today brought back in to test it out if they agree to it, that is, just to make it easier," Dr. Irlum tells us. "Since we already have all the information needed for them, it'll be good to compare the two."

"Okay."

That means that Riley will be getting called back in, and I'll get to see her again. I had wanted to ask her for her number or ask to see her again, but I chickened out. I guess there's a pattern in that regard. Instead of asking her anything, I just stood there watching her get into the back of a cab from the doorway of the building.

And because you can never be too safe and never know what type of cab driver you'll get, I also took note of the cab's license plate, just in case. Having it made me feel better.

I'm so glad she didn't run off on me during lunch. I was so horrified that she thought I was using her to avoid another woman. I couldn't even blame her for thinking that because she doesn't know me at all. It hadn't even crossed my mind that Maya might be interested in me, but after that encounter, it made me think of all the times she's lingered around or how she always tries to talk to me or get my attention. I'm still not too sure, though. She's probably just being friendly.

The rest of my workday is uneventful compared to the morning and lunch, but I'm left feeling antsy and unsettled after seeing Riley again. That's probably why I completely surprise both Patrick and myself when I actually accept his invitation to grab some dinner together after work. I meet him at a steakhouse not too far from where we work, and we settle into one of the back booths.

"So, listen." He leans in while cutting up his steak. "There's this experimental procedure I'm hoping to try real soon."

"Yeah?"

He nods. "But, you know, with the risks it involves, it's hard to find any volunteers. Plus, they need to meet a certain criteria."

"What type of risks?"

He takes a bite of his steak, chewing and swallowing before answering. "Well, if something were to go wrong, there's a possibility of permanent blindness." He dabs a napkin on his lips. "There's also the risk of causing a more severe case of blindness than they already have."

I contemplate that as I start eating my own food. I'm not sure how I would feel about getting it done, and I'm not sure I'd want anyone I cared about to have it done, either. I know Patrick is good at what he does, but as he said, it's experimental.

He starts talking about it some more, but my mind drifts to Riley. I wonder if she's ever had any procedures done to her. She said she wasn't always blind, which means there was some sort of accident in her past that caused it. I guess there's also the chance it was caused by a disease.

An elbow jabbing lightly into my arm brings me out of my head. "I'm probably boring you with all this talk, huh?" Patrick asks with a smile. "I just get excited about it."

"Sorry. It's not boring. I was just thinking."

He shrugs and continues on talking about something else as we continue eating our food.

Patrick and I don't linger for too long after eating, so it's still fairly early when we leave the steakhouse. I drive all the way home to my townhouse, but then when I arrive, I end up just sitting in my car, staring ahead. I don't feel like being in there alone, where it's quiet except for my neighbor's TV, that I can hear through our joined wall.

I contemplate calling my parents but decide against it. You'd think that with my brother gone, they would be in contact with me a lot more and make more of an effort with me. But, no. If anything, they've talked to me even less. And they've never even been here to see where I live, even though I've suggested they come for a visit.

I reverse back out of my parking spot and drive to The Reading Nook instead. I don't usually go there on Mondays, but after today, I just kind of *want* to be there.

After walking through the doors, I start heading towards

my usual seat, only to trip on my own feet when I see Riley sitting in my favorite spot.

What is she doing here? And why do I keep running into her?

Rather than saying hello to her, since she might get creeped out and think that I'm following her or something, I choose a seat that's opposite her and lower myself into the chair.

I'm confused at first when I see her holding a book open in front of her. But then I notice that it's upside down, and she's also wearing earbuds. It must be an audiobook, and I'm guessing that maybe holding a book makes her feel like she's reading it instead of just listening to it.

I can't help but watch as she occasionally turns the pages as if she's following along. My heart hurts at the thought of what she's lost and what she has to do now to deal with it.

She looks beautiful with her hair piled on top of her head in a messy bun. And she's wearing a cute dress that ends just above her knees. Her shoes are matching, and I briefly wonder if she has some sort of system for them to make sure she always has a pair that go together.

When I realize that I'm bordering on the line of unacceptable social behavior by simply sitting and staring at her, I force myself to look away. I pull my book out and glue my eyes to the page. It works for a few minutes, too, that is, until I hear a clattering of noise followed by a curse.

Looking up, I see that Riley's bag has dropped to the ground, and items from inside it have spilled out and scattered around. I get to my feet instantly, throwing my book behind me as I rush over to her. She drops to her knees at the same time I get there.

"Here, let me help," I say, crouching down.

"JD?" she questions.

"Yes. How did you know?" When I glance at her, I see that she has a few tears lining her eyes. It causes an ache in my chest.

"I've become good at recognizing voices over the past while." She feels around the ground for her items, but I stop her hand.

"Let me. You sit back in the chair."

Riley sighs but then hauls herself back up into the chair while I gather her things and start placing them back into her bag. The sound of sniffling has my head whipping back to look at her.

"Are you okay?" I ask.

She lets out a watery laugh through her tears. "Yeah. All I wanted was a drink from my water bottle, but I couldn't feel it in my bag when I searched through it. So I went to put my bag back on the chair next to me, but I didn't realize my earbud cord had caught on the zipper. It yanked out of my ear and kind of surprised me, and I ended up fumbling everything, and my bag dropped." She swipes a tear away from under her eye. "I think I broke my earbuds as well."

I look in my hands at said earbuds and see that the cord is indeed snapped. I don't know what to do about that, but I know that I don't like seeing her cry.

"I'm sorry," I tell her.

"No. I'm sorry," she says, leaning her head back and waving her hands over her eyes like she's drying them. "I'm just having a moment. It's happened a lot during this pregnancy." She blows out a long breath and turns toward me. "There. Moment over."

I smile and move to sit on the seat next to her. "Here. I found your water." I place the bottle into her hand.

"Thanks." She takes a drink and puts the lid back on. "Everything is just so hard when you can't see. I feel like I can't do anything."

"I can't imagine," I say. "Here's your bag, and yes, I'm sorry, but your earbuds are broken."

After a groan, she says, "Of course they are. Ugh. Thanks for your help. What are you doing here anyway? You're not following me, are you?"

I scan her face for any sign that she's serious. But there doesn't appear to be any type of concern on her face. In fact, the very edges of her mouth curve up just the slightest bit.

"No, not following you." My own lips lift in return. "I just came to read."

"I guess that was a dumb question, asking why you're here." She shakes her head. "That's literally why people come here. So, you like to read?"

"I do."

She smiles and then tilts her head to the side in thought. "Would you maybe... oh, never mind."

"What?"

"Well, I, uh. I was going to ask if you'd maybe read to me, but it's silly. Don't worry, forget I said anything."

I'm equal parts surprised and happy that she would ask me to do that. It means that she's feeling comfortable enough with me.

"Okay."

"JD, it's okay. You don't have–"

"It's fine," I say, cutting her off. "I don't mind."

I can't say I've ever been asked to read to anyone before. I certainly don't usually speak with anybody as much as I do with her. The only other person that I felt comfortable like this with was Shay.

"Are you sure?" Riley asks and then smiles. "I have to warn you. It's a romance book."

I chuckle softly at the same time I feel the tips of my ears heat. I've never read a romance before, but I'm sure it can't be that bad, can it?

"Yes, I'm sure."

Riley chews on her bottom lip for a moment, and I find myself staring at it the whole time she does. Then she nods. "Okay, thank you, JD." She hands over the same book she had in her hand when I arrived. "I was in chapter four, but I wasn't too far in. You can just start at the beginning of the chapter again. Please."

And so, I begin to read. I read to this beautiful woman that I first saw on Friday, met again today, performed an ultrasound on her, and then had lunch with. I *should* feel odd about it, but I don't. I just wish she didn't look so much like Shay so I could know for sure whether I'm feeling this way because of her or if it's simply because she looks the same.

The book I'm reading is about a man and woman who get together while they were each away on a trip, and then for whatever reason, they didn't exchange numbers. I guess it was explained in the earlier chapters. I can't help but think about how much that part reminds me of Shay and I. Although, in this book, they end up working at the same place several months later.

The longer I read, the more relaxed Riley gets. So relaxed, that she ends up falling asleep. Her head somehow ended up on my shoulder at some point, and I didn't bother moving it. I close the book and look down at her soft features. She really is gorgeous.

I let my eyes drift further down to her stomach. I've seen many pregnant bellies of all shapes and sizes. But for some reason, I find her belly to be particularly adorable.

I turn away when a touch of guilt hits me. Even though she told me she didn't want to know what she was having, I looked. I know that she's having a boy because I specifically searched for it, and I probably shouldn't have.

Riley stirs next to me. "Did I fall asleep?"

I offer a small smile. "Yes."

"Sorry." She stretches out. "I guess I should get home. Can you tell me what the time is?"

I check my watch. "It's almost nine-thirty."

"Oh, wow, okay, yeah. I need to get home."

I hand over her book and then double-check that all of her things are in her bag and none are left on the floor.

"Let me just grab my stuff, and then I can take you home."

"Oh, are you sure?" she asks. "I can get a cab."

"I'm sure. I would rather take you than send you in a cab late at night."

"You sound like my sister." She chuckles softly. "But thank you. I appreciate it. And thank you for reading to me."

"You're welcome."

I grab all of my stuff and then place Riley's hand on my arm before leading her out. She gives me the address, and then once we arrive, I watch to make sure she gets into the building safely.

CHAPTER NINE

Riley

I take a seat at the breakfast bar in Mia's kitchen and then instantly feel the need to pee.

Again.

"Dammit." Groaning, I stand up again. "I need to use the bathroom. I'll be right back."

"Do you want any help?"

"Nope," I say, popping the p and waving her off.

Another thing I love about Mia is that she'll offer to help, but she doesn't insist on helping me like I'm incapable of doing things by myself.

"You know where it is then."

Mia, like my sister, cleared up anything that may be an obstacle for me so that I could still walk around their houses without worrying too much. Once I'm back on my stool, Mia nudges my mug filled with tea against my hand, and I wrap my fingers around it.

"Thanks," I say, lifting it to my lips.

"So, what have you been up to, Shay-Shay?" Ever since our trip, the name has kind of stuck, and she's been calling me that regularly. Only her, though.

"Oh, you know how crazy my life gets these days. Sprinkle in a Doctor's appointment here, and a touch of answering the phone at my sister's restaurant there." She hums while I run my fingers over the handle of my mug. And because I usually tell her everything, I add, "Actually, after my ultrasound the other day, I had lunch with a guy."

Her response is instant. "What?! Who?!"

"Um, it was the guy who did my ultrasound."

She's quiet for a moment, and I wonder if she's thinking the same thing as my sister. Hell, even I was starting to think the same thing as my sister. That is until JD and I crossed paths again at The Reading Nook.

"He wasn't some old pervert, was he?"

I can't help but laugh at her words. Trust her to say something like that. "According to Sheryl at the cafe, he was a very handsome guy."

"Oooooh," she sing-songs. "But, unfortunately, you can't always go by what Sheryl says about stuff like that."

I lift my tea for another sip. Unfortunately, she's right. "That's true. You can't. But he did have a really nice voice. He didn't sound old, and he didn't sound ugly."

"Do ugly guys sound different?" she ponders, and I laugh.

"I have no idea," I say with a smile. "His skin felt nice too, definitely not old."

"You touched him? You hussy!"

"Calm down. He offered his arm to me when we crossed the street."

"Aw, that's actually kind of sweet."

"Yeah." I take another sip of my tea. "Actually, there was a woman from his work who approached us while we were waiting for our food. She was definitely interested in him. I kind of accused him of using me to escape her."

"What did he say to that?" Mia asks, and I can hear the humor in her voice.

"He sounded pretty insulted but more so upset that I'd think that. I felt bad."

She chuckles. "Well, you are a little more sensitive right now, and for a good reason. You have extra hormones running through your body."

I hear her rummaging around in the kitchen before she comes and sits down next to me. I turn my body more in her direction.

"You know the weird thing, though? He feels really familiar to me. He actually reminds me of Jasper."

"Gosh, could you imagine? That would be crazy if it were him."

"Yeah, except it's not him. It can't be. He would have definitely said something for sure." That's assuming that our night was as memorable to him as it was to me.

"But, what if–"

The front door opens and closes with a loud bang. "Hey, babe!" her husband, Kyone, calls out. "I was thinking we could get naked before dinner, then I can lick..." he trails off when I assume he sees me. "Shit," he curses from somewhere closer. "Sorry, Riley. I didn't know you were here."

He kisses my cheek, and I watch as his big dark shadowy figure moves to stand next to Mia. "I feel weird about you kissing my cheek right after saying that."

He chuckles. "Pretend you heard nothing."

"Heard what?" I go to nudge him with my elbow and thankfully make contact with his arm. "How was basketball? That's where you were, right?" I ask.

"Yeah, it was good. The kids are definitely a lot better than a few weeks back. Man, it was painful to watch."

"I'll bet." I smile. Kyone coaches kid's basketball after school and apparently started off with some pretty bad players this time. "I should get going now so you guys can eat, or, you know...lick...your plates."

Kyone elbows me this time. "Nah, why don't you stay for dinner?"

"Yeah, Shay-Shay, don't leave me alone with him."

I'm pretty sure Mia just kissed him after saying that. I know she loves him more than anything, and Kyone loves her just as much, if not more. I'm not gonna lie. I'm kind of jealous of their love.

"It's okay. I don't really like being out late anyway. Thank you, though."

The dark can be kind of scary, actually, because I can't see any of the shadows around me that I normally would during the day. Everything is just...black. I'm glad JD had taken me home the other night. It was odd for me to be out at night alone, but after the conversation with my sister, I just wanted to be.

"Okay, if you're sure. I'll order you an uber and walk you down."

"Thanks, girl," I say to her. "See ya, Kyone."

"Bye, Riley."

He hugs me before I turn and get my shoes on, and then

Mia and I chat until my ride pulls up in front of us.

"I'll text ya tomorrow," I say, sliding into the car.

"Um, no. You'll text when you get home. Nothing about those rules has changed, miss independent."

I roll my eyes. "You know, I would have. I just meant I'll text after my shift tomorrow at the restaurant, and we'll figure out dinner for Saturday night."

"Okay, hon. Bye."

"See ya."

I realize on the way home that I didn't mention to Mia about my second encounter with JD at The Reading Nook. I didn't tell my sister about it either. Maybe it was intentional. Maybe I just want to keep the memory all to myself.

It was a nice night, and he was so sweet. I didn't want them wrecking the memory with their worries and opinions. Not that Mia would have necessarily done that, but my sister definitely would have. Just because I'm blind and pregnant doesn't mean I can't make friends and spend time with men, or one man in particular, especially when I get that gut feeling that I'm safe around him.

After listening to my baby's heartbeat in bed, I fall asleep to thoughts of JD reading to me.

The following morning, I wake up to the sound of my phone ringing. Alexa informs me that it's the clinic where I had my ultrasound done. At first, I'm consumed with worry, thinking that they're calling because something is wrong with the baby. But then that worry shifts to excitement when I start thinking that maybe it's *him* calling.

"Hello?"

"Is this Riley Brooks?" a woman asks. My emotions are like a see-saw, with worry rising again since it's not his voice.

"Yes, that's me," I answer, sitting up against the headboard of my bed.

"Hi, Riley. I'm calling from *Your Health Imaging center*. I'm calling because we have a new program that we're testing out, and we wanted to know if you were willing to come back in for another ultrasound for comparing purposes?"

"Oh, um, is there a reason that I'm specifically being asked to come in for it?"

I can hear the clicking of a keyboard through the phone. "We're actually calling everyone that was here on Monday. Since we have the information from you already, we can compare the data."

"Even if time has passed?" I'm no doctor, but even I know that just a week in pregnancy can mean big changes to the baby.

"Yes. If you come in on Monday, then it will be exactly a week. We can work with the weeks' difference."

I rub circles on my belly. "Okay, sure. If it's safe, two ultrasounds close together, I mean."

"I can assure you it's completely safe for both you and your baby."

"Alright, sure. So, Monday?" I was supposed to be going to the restaurant for work, but it's not a big deal if I don't, or I could just go in after.

"Thank you. Yes, Monday at the same time as your previous appointment, eleven forty-five. Does that work?"

"Yes, I can be there then."

"Great," she answers cheerfully. "We'll see you then. Enjoy the rest of your day."

"Thank you, you too. Bye."

I need to make my way to the bathroom as soon as I hang up because this little baby is pressing onto my bladder. And then, once I get out of the bathroom, I make sure to get

Alexa to add my appointment to my calendar.

JD and I never planned to meet up again, and we still never exchanged numbers, so I wasn't really sure if I'd see him again. But if I have to go back there to get another ultrasound, then he may very well be the one to perform it. A little spark of hope floats around me and lands on my face in the form of a smile.

There's a certain type of peace he gives me just by being around him. So if we can at least become friends, then I'll be happy. That may be what my gut is trying to tell me; that we both need each other as friends.

"Alexa, what time is it?"

"The time is eight twenty-two A.M."

I guess it's time to start getting ready to go to the restaurant.

CHAPTER TEN

Jasper

On Friday, when I leave work for the weekend, I'm feeling pretty good. After saying goodbye to Riley on Monday night, I wasn't sure when I'd be seeing her again. But I knew that I could always get her information from work if I really wanted. It isn't exactly appropriate, but the option is there.

The thought of inquiring about her from the woman at the cafe where we had lunch at had crossed my mind as well since she seemed to know her.

In the end, I don't have to do either of those things because she'll be coming in again on Monday for another appointment. And I'll be the one taking care of it.

As per usual, I head to The Reading Nook straight from work. I get settled into my usual seat and then start reading. About twenty minutes later, I glance up from my book to see

Riley walking toward me. My heart instantly skips a beat and then starts beating faster.

She ends up sitting on a seat opposite me and then takes a moment to rub her belly. I sit mesmerized, watching her hand move.

Even though I know she can't see me here, I still have the briefest, irrational moment of hurt that she didn't say hello.

I snap myself back to reality and speak up. "Hey, Riley."

She startles a little. "JD?"

"Yeah." I get up and join her, sitting down on the seat next to her.

She smiles. "I take it you must come here often since this is the second time that I've run into you here this week."

"Yeah, I've been coming pretty often for the past few months," I say. "What about you?"

Her smile turns a little sad. "I used to come here to read all the time before the accident."

"I'm sorry."

She shrugs. "It is what it is."

It must be so hard to go from seeing everything and living your life normally and then having something happen and losing your sight. Everything you once knew would be suddenly changed.

"Did you bring a book today?" I ask.

"Yeah. I don't know why, though." She laughs at herself. "I haven't bought new headphones yet, so I can't even listen to it."

"I can read to you again," I blurt out before I can think twice. There's something about her that has me behaving differently whenever she's around. Not to mention talking more.

"Really?" She smiles brightly in my direction. "I would love that. Are you sure?"

"Yes."

"Okay. Thank you, JD."

Riley hands over her book and leans back in the chair, resting her hands on the top of her bump. I spend the next hour reading to her, stealing quick glances at her every few minutes. But when I hear a loud grumbling sound that isn't from me, I realize that she probably hasn't eaten any dinner yet. I haven't either, but she's eating for two, so I want to make sure she's fed.

"You're hungry," I state while closing the book.

"I am," she replies with a small smile. "I guess I should get going and go eat some dinner."

As she starts to shuffle herself to the edge of the chair, I ask, "Would you like to have dinner with me?" I usually just grab some takeout on the way home after being here on a Friday, but I would go somewhere with her if she wanted.

She pauses and looks in my direction. "Honestly, I would... but JD, I have to ask. Doesn't it bother you about my situation?"

"You're situation?"

She waves her hand at her stomach and face. "You know, my sight and being pregnant."

"No," I answer immediately because it's the truth. "Does it bother you?"

She seems taken aback by my answer and starts rubbing her belly, my eyes tracking the movements again. "No. Well, sort of, I guess. I just... I'm not exactly a catch, JD. Even if I could see, I'm... well, I'm carrying another man's child. I guess I'm just wondering what it is that you want from me?"

A weird feeling of jealousy sparks in me when she mentions carrying another man's baby, but I try to push it away. I barely know this woman and shouldn't be having feelings like that. Still, I can't help but wonder what kind of a man would ditch a pregnant woman and leave her to do all of this by herself. Not a very good one. I guess I don't really know what the story is between her and her possible ex. I just know that he's not here.

Nerves skitter inside my stomach as I think of my answer. "I think you're a beautiful woman," I say quietly. "And I'd just like to get to know you better. At least maybe become friends." Then I hold my breath as I wait for her response.

What I said seems to do the trick because a gorgeous smile slowly spreads across her face. "Okay." She nods. "That would be nice."

Relief washes over me. I look her over again, my eyes wanting to soak in her beauty, soak in the strength that I can see in her, and the vulnerability I can sense from her as well.

I take her hand in mine. "Ready to go?"

"Sure." She gives my hand a squeeze. "Where would you like to go?"

"Is the baby craving anything?" I ask.

Riley hums for a moment. "The baby would love tacos." She sighs. "But tacos are really messy, which is bad when you can't see them."

Every time she talks about things she can no longer do or is afraid to do, I find myself wanting to prove that she can, for the most part, still do them. "Have you ever had taco wraps before?"

"What are those?" she asks as we stand and gather our things.

"They're something I make. Instead of putting all of your stuff into a taco, you put it into a wrap and crumble the taco shell into it."

"Mm, that sounds delicious."

"It is," I say, placing her hand in the crook of my elbow. "I can make it for you if you like?"

She hesitates a moment. "Maybe it would be better if we just eat out somewhere this time."

I realize that I just inadvertently asked her to come back to my place when she doesn't even really know me. "Sorry, I didn't even think. Of course, we can go somewhere else." I'm glad she's being cautious with her safety. It's not just her that she has to worry about, but the baby boy she's carrying as well.

"You don't need to apologize, JD. To be honest, my gut tells me that I'm safe with you. But maybe we get to know each other a little more first. Okay?"

I smile. "Yes. That's fine." I guide her out of the building and toward my car. "I don't really eat out very often, so we can go wherever you like."

"Hmm. There's an Italian restaurant a couple of blocks from here called Ragazzi's. I could go for some gnocchi."

"I take it you've been there before?" I ask, opening the passenger door for her.

"Yeah. I've lived here my whole life, so I've pretty much been everywhere."

"Okay, Ragazzi's it is."

Only once we're seated at a table in this cozy little restaurant do I start to feel the fluttering in the pit of my stomach from being here with her. I'm supposed to be looking at the menu, but I was suddenly struck with the realization that this is a date of sorts. I think I've actually been doing okay with the small talk with her so far, but now I'm at a loss for words and don't know what to say next.

I hadn't counted our lunch together the other day as a date, so I didn't feel the same nervousness. Something about the daylight, the noise, and the casualness of the cafe, made it easy not to think about. But here... here there are little tea-light candles on each table. It's nighttime. And there are only quiet murmurs from the other people enjoying their dinners, creating a romantic atmosphere.

"Do you know what you want?" Riley asks after another moment.

I, of course, spent the last minute or so watching the orange glow from the flames against her face instead of looking at the menu. I quickly swing my eyes back to the food listed and pick out the first thing I see. "The chicken pesto linguine."

"Mm, good choice."

When I don't say anything more, she tilts her head to the side with her eyes fixed on me, a curious expression on her face. I have no idea what she's thinking. I'm even more confused when she smiles and shakes her head, looking back toward the flames, but I don't ask her what that's about.

I can't remember the last time I was on a date. Besides that night with Shay, which wasn't even a date exactly, it's been years. That's kind of embarrassing, really. And if I don't want to die alone like my brother, then I need to make more of an effort in the dating department.

Every time I've thought about dating over the past while, though, I've felt anxious and uncomfortable. The thought of putting myself out there in front of a stranger has sweat breaking out on my body most of the time.

I know I've had opportunities, but my mind has always gone back to thoughts of Shay. That is, until Riley. I haven't wanted to try to make something work with anyone else as I have with her. But hell, she looks like Shay's double.

My eyes trail over her face as she stares at the candles on the table with a soft smile on her lips. Her bright blue eyes which are slightly cloudy, are the color of the sky on a clear day. Her lips are a natural pinkish-red color, with the lower lip plumper than the top, both still nice and full. She has absolutely no makeup on, but she looks absolutely perfect.

For some reason, that thought has me realizing that it's *her* that I want. *This* woman that I'm drawn to. This sweet, strong, pregnant woman. I need to close the chapter that I've kept a finger in for the past five months now. I need to turn the page and see where this thing with Riley will go. I need to step out of my comfort zone and put in real effort. Hopefully, she's willing to see where this leads us as well.

CHAPTER ELEVEN

Riley

Once the waiter takes our orders, I return my eyes to the brightness of the candles on the table. It's dim in here, so unfortunately, I can't see the shadows of most of the things surrounding us. Whenever I've spoken to JD, I simply look to where I hope his face is.

The flames, though... the flames I can kind of see, so I've kept my sights on them.

Since we arrived here, JD has been even more quiet than usual and has been giving me shorter answers. It reminds me of Jasper and how he was the night that we were together. So, now I've been sitting here thinking about Jasper *instead* of JD, the extremely kind man across from me with the nice – okay, *sexy* – voice. And I feel guilty about that.

It's kind of hard not to think about Jasper, though, when

I have his baby pressing up against my bladder most of the time.

JD has seemed mostly okay with me until now, so maybe he's just nervous or something? I mean, it's not like he's been the most chattiest person to begin with, but he has read a romance novel to me, for goodness sake, so he *shouldn't* be nervous around me.

Okay, enough of this, I need to focus on *him*, and I need to draw him out again.

"If you wrote a novel, what type would it be?" I blurt. "Mystery? Horror? Romance?"

He's quiet for a moment and then finally answers, "Well, I don't think I could write a romance." I can hear a small smile in his voice, and it has me relaxing a little. "Mystery, probably. That's what I usually like to read." He pauses. "What about you?"

"Hmm, I'd probably write a romance since that's what I read." I smile. "Well, listen to. I guess I can't actually write either."

"Do you read braille at all?"

I sigh. "I'm still learning. After I lost my sight, it took a while for me to finally accept that this is my life and that I needed to start learning things like that."

"May I ask how you lost your sight?"

"A car accident. Someone went through a stop sign and t-boned me." I get lost in the memories of that day. How I was on the phone with my sister, telling her I was pregnant. The sounds of metal crunching and the screeching of tires.

"I'm sorry," JD says, bringing me back.

I shrug in response, then feel in front of me for my glass of water. Immediately, I feel his warm hands on mine, guiding them. The reaction I get from him touching me manages to erase any thoughts of Jasper that had surfaced earlier, especially when he continues to hold his hands over mine, even after my fingers are wrapped firmly around the glass.

They're a lot bigger than mine, and for some reason, an intense feeling of being protected and cared for passes through his fingers to mine. I always thought that when there were sparks between people that it was more of a feeling of attraction, but this right now feels like literal sparks zapping from his fingers to mine, and it makes little flutters appear in my stomach.

JD finally releases my hand, and I lift the glass of water to my lips to take a big sip. My mouth is suddenly feeling quite dry now.

I clear my throat. "How was work today?"

"It was good." After a beat, he alters his answer like he's trying to be more conversational. "I mean, it was pretty good. There was a woman who is pregnant with triplets who came in. So that's always incredible to see. All girls."

"Oh my goodness." I laugh. "She is going to be busy!"

"I feel sorry for the dad. His eyes kind of glazed over when I told them what they were having."

I laugh softly again while absently rubbing over my belly. "Teenage years won't be fun for him." I grin.

After that, it seems like the air around us is much lighter, and we're able to talk a lot more freely again. He elaborates on his answers and asks me questions too. I don't think he finds small talk to be easy, so I've tried to stick mostly to my random questions about random things.

We end up sharing our food with each other, and I make sure to stay eating above my plate so that I don't make a mess of myself and the area around my plate without knowing.

As our plates are being taken away and we've both

decided against dessert, JD speaks up again. "Can I ask you something?"

"Sure."

"I hope this doesn't upset you. But what do you miss most about being able to see? If that's too much to ask–"

"No. No, it's fine." I think for a moment. "I don't know if there is any *one* thing. I miss seeing the sun shining on a warm day. I miss seeing colors; colorful clothes, colorful flowers. I miss seeing people's faces and being able to read their facial expressions. I miss how easy everything was. You don't realize until it's gone how much you took it for granted and how there are so many things you can no longer do." He stays quiet, and I feel like I've maybe made it sound really depressing, so I add, "But I've learned to enjoy the sounds around me more, to enjoy the feel of the sun on my skin instead. I've learned to listen to the words *not* being spoken by those around me, as well as everything in between. And I listen to the *way* people speak. I've learned to use my imagination more, and I imagine all the colors around me." I smile. "And I enjoy touches from people a lot more."

I feel his hand slip on top of mine on the table. "I think... I think that's incredible. You're incredible."

I feel a warmth spread in my chest at his words. Nobody talks to me about this stuff. It's like they're too afraid of upsetting me or something, so they tip-toe around the subject.

"What would you be doing this weekend if you could see?"

"Hmm, well, let me think." I laugh a little. "I'd eat tacos. Go bowling. Watch a movie at the cinemas, and then go dancing. Although bowling and dancing might have been a little hard with this." I gesture to my stomach. "But I think I could have pulled it off."

I listen as the waiter must give JD the check, and he pays

it.

"I think you can still do all of that. I mean, who cares if eating tacos is messy? And someone could help you with bowling. As far as movies go, you could always just listen to one. You listen to books, right? And all you need is someone with you to be able to dance as well." A moment later, he softly adds, "We should do it."

"What do you mean?"

"Let's do it. Well, maybe not all of it this weekend. I–I could pick you up to go bowling on Sunday. We could try out the others another day."

I stare at what I think is his face.

"What?" he asks when I don't say anything for a while. I can hear the uncertainty in his voice.

"It's just... I think that's the most you've said to me in one go. Well, except for when you were reading to me, but that doesn't count." He chuckles softly, and I like the sound of it *a lot*. It fills me with a warm fuzzy feeling. "You have a nice laugh, by the way," I say quietly. "As for Sunday... well, that sounds nice too."

It really doesn't seem to bother him that I'm pregnant, so I've decided to try not to let it bother me, either.

"Yeah?" he asks, needing confirmation.

"Yes."

"Okay," he responds. "I can pick you up at five, so we're not out too late."

I smile widely at him and nod as excitement burrows its way into my body. I can feel it everywhere. At this moment, I wish I could see his face, just to see if excitement is dancing in his eyes as well. To see if there is a flush to his cheeks like I think there might be. Although the actual words he said were like a regular person making plans, I could still hear the nervousness in his voice that he tried to cover up, and I find that endearing.

I think non-cocky nice guys are my thing now. I've known too many assholes in my life, and I'm done with them. I guess I have been for a while now.

As more time passes, I'm unable to stop a yawn from passing through my lips. Right away, I hear a chair scrape back.

"Come on," JD says. "It's getting late. I'll drive you home."

"Thanks, it just sort of hit me now how tired I am."

A second later, I feel his hand slip into mine to help me up. I expect him to let go once I'm standing, but he doesn't. He leads me out into the night air, holding my hand, and I relish every second of his warmth enveloping me. I enjoy feeling every groove of his palm, the softness mixed with the roughness.

But then, all too quickly, it's gone.

"Here we are," he says, as I hear the sound of unlocking followed by a car door opening.

The ride home is quiet, but it's in no way awkward. I listen to the sounds of the engine as it speeds up and slows down. I listen to the gentle rhythm of the indicator when we turn a corner. And the occasional *thump* of the tires hitting a pothole.

I was never afraid to get back in a vehicle after the accident. That turned out to be a blessing since walking everywhere wasn't exactly a good option for me. I haven't even thought about what I'm going to do once the baby is born. I guess I'll have to carry a car seat with me everywhere for the cab ride.

When we arrive at my building, I accept his offer to walk me to the door. Even though I know in my heart that JD is a good guy, I still discreetly check for that big round planter with the cracked concrete underneath to make sure I'm at the right building. I knew I'd find it.

JD doesn't try to come in or kiss me goodnight when we arrive at my door. And I can't tell if I'm relieved or disappointed by it. I decide to settle on feeling happy that he's being a gentleman and not trying to rush anything.

I have the biggest smile on my face as I go through the steps of getting ready for sleep, and then once I'm in bed, I drift off to thoughts about what his lips might feel like.

CHAPTER TWELVE

Riley

"Alexa, what time is it?"

"The time is four forty-six P.M."

I blow out another nervous breath, tapping my fingers on my thigh. Why am I so nervous? No, not nervous. *Anxious.* All day I've been waiting for five o'clock to come around. Actually, that's not true. I've been waiting since Friday night after JD dropped me off.

Even last night, when I was out at dinner with Mia and our other friend Chelsea, who was in town for only one night, I was distracted by thinking about this date. Luckily I was able to hide it well, and my friends didn't seem to notice.

As I sit here counting down the minutes, apprehension starts to take over my thoughts. What if he's realized that he doesn't want to hang out with a pregnant woman after all? What if he's decided that my being blind is too much work for him? What if–

A knock sounds loudly throughout my apartment.

I walk quickly over to my front door and lean my head against it. "Who is it?" I ask.

"It's JD."

I smile immediately. I guess that answers my questions as to whether or not he's decided I'm more trouble than I'm worth.

"Hey," I say, opening the door. I can see his shadow standing there, but he doesn't say anything right away. "JD?"

He clears his throat. "Sorry. You... you look beautiful."

I can feel the heat hit my cheeks, and I push some hair behind my ears. "Thank you. I'm sure you look handsome." I grin and then step aside. "Do you want to come in for a moment? I just need to grab my bag and cane."

"Sure." He steps in and closes the door behind him. "I, ah, got you something. Two somethings, actually."

"You did?" I ask as I reach the couch where my bag is.

"Yeah, here." He passes me two items. "I got you some new headphones and a tactile tic-tac-toe. I'm not sure if you even like tic-tac-toe, but I just thought... you know what, it's stupid. I'll just take that back."

I feel his hands land on the package, but I yank it back. "No! That's so incredibly thoughtful. I love it. Thank you so much, JD." It truly is such a sweet and thoughtful thing for him to do.

Several seconds pass before he quietly says, "You're welcome."

I feel those damn pregnancy hormones making an appearance again. So instead of hugging him like I really want to, I make an excuse about needing to use the bathroom before we leave. Really, it's just to give me a minute to get my emotions under control so he doesn't see me cry. Then, since I'm in here anyway, I do end up peeing.

When I come out, I pick up my bag. "Ready?"

"Are you okay?" he asks in reply.

It hadn't even occurred to me that my eyes are probably red or glassy. I was hoping that my little tear-up wouldn't show. "I'm perfect." I smile, choosing to ignore how I might look.

"Okay then." He doesn't press the issue but takes hold of my hand and leads us down to his car.

His palm is slightly sweaty, so I'm guessing I'm not the only one who's feeling something about our date. That actually helps settle my own nerves and makes my confidence rise again. I used to be more confident and carefree, but things changed after the accident.

We arrive at the bowling alley, and the unmistakable sounds of balls rolling along and knocking down pins hit my ears. I find myself smiling again. I'm not exactly sure how this is going to work, but I'm excited about trying it out regardless.

We get our shoes, and JD leads me over to our lane and seats. Once I make sure that I have my shoes the right way, I put them on.

"You shouldn't use a really heavy ball, so try this one," JD says, handing me one.

It's definitely lighter than what I've used in the past, but I'm sure I can work with it. "It's good, thank you."

"I figure we can play our first round and then eat. Then we can decide if we want to play another round after that. Unless you're hungry now?"

"No. I'm okay," I tell him. "It sounds like a good plan."

"Okay."

He appears to be more at ease than he was when we went for dinner the other night, so that's good.

I manage to stand up, feeling like I'm carrying two balls now. One in my stomach and one in my hand. Then I laugh at the fact that I was thinking about two balls, which of course, takes me back to the last time I held *those* types of balls, and they were–

"Are you ready?" JD asks, interrupting my line of thought.

"Yep. Lead the way."

Since I'm holding the ball in my hands, I expect him to grab my elbow to guide me. Instead, I'm surprised when I feel his hands land on my waist. I'm sure I let out a little gasp at the contact, but I don't know if he notices. I'm wearing jeans with a stretchy waistband and one of my favorite loose tops from when I was able to see, but the heat from his hands makes it feel like they're sitting directly on my bare skin.

"Is this okay?" he asks. All I can do is nod, and then he guides me toward the lane. "There's a step in front of you." He grips my waist tighter to stop me from continuing on and waits for me to take the step. I close my eyes for a second, enjoying the feel of his hands on me and the closeness of his body, then I take the step. "Okay, we're at the fault line. You're facing directly down the middle, so you're good to go," he says, releasing me.

I nod, bring the ball up in front of me first, then swing it back and then forward, letting it go when I feel the time is right, just like I used to. I listen to the ball roll along and then hear it surprisingly hit some pins.

"You knocked four down," JD says from beside me.

I let out a little squeal and then turn to hug his blurry shadow. Happy emotions overwhelm me. I never thought that I would be able to do anything like this again, and I'm so appreciative to JD for bringing me here and doing this for me.

"Thank you so much for this."

JD wraps his arms around my back, and I swear I feel a shiver run through his body as he leans into me further.

"You're welcome." He pulls back a second later. "I'll get your next ball. Wait here."

A moment later, he places another, or maybe it's the same ball, in my hands. I hit another two pins, and I couldn't be happier. JD guides me by the waist to the seats even though I'm not holding a ball this time. I think he just likes touching me, but I don't mind it one bit.

He goes to take his turn, but from where I'm sitting, I'm not sure if the sounds are from our lane or the one next to us.

When I see his shadow sit down next to me again, I ask, "How many did you hit?"

He hesitates for a moment before answering. "I got a strike."

There's something odd about his voice that has me frowning. He's not telling the truth, and then it dawns on me. "You got a gutter ball, didn't you?" I laugh. "You didn't hit anything either time, you sneaky bastard!"

I hear him chuckle softly. "I just wanted to see what your reaction was going to be. I would have told you the truth after that."

"Mhmm, I'm not going to believe you now." I'm smiling so widely my cheeks hurt. It feels so good to be joking around rather than being babied and making everything about my blindness so serious. It's like he knows I just want to be treated as normal as possible.

"This is only my second time bowling," he says, helping

me up for my next turn.

"Really?"

"Yes. The first time was in college. I didn't... get a chance before that."

JD hands me a ball and then guides me by the waist again. It might just be my imagination, but it feels like he holds me closer to him this time.

We continue on this way for the rest of the game, chatting between bowls. After the first few turns, I started to be able to tell when pins in our lane were being knocked over, as opposed to the lane next to us. So I always knew when JD knocked over pins and when he didn't. I enjoyed making fun of him for being beaten by a blind person, and he chuckled softly at the look of sheer concentration I apparently got on my face before each bowl.

By the end of our game, JD told me the score was thirty-nine for him and fifty-eight for me. Terrible scores, really, but the most fun I've had in a long while.

We order some food, and then I ask JD to lead me to the separate accessible toilet restroom since they're easier for me to use.

"Um, can you tell me if it's clean?" I ask, slightly embarrassed.

Thankfully, JD doesn't seem bothered by my question at all. I think we've both been feeling more and more comfortable with each other as the night has gone on.

"It's pretty clean. The toilet is to your right in the corner, and the sink is right next to it."

"Thank you," I tell him. "You don't have to wait."

"I'll go wash my hands and wait at the end of the hall."

"Okay."

I do what I need to do and then wash my hands. Going to

the bathroom in a public place is just one more thing that I've had to get used to doing over time. I usually use my cane to feel for the toilet, and I always use little wipes that I carry with me to wipe everything over before I sit down. I'd probably throw up if I were to sit on someone else's pee or even just something wet in general when I have no clue what it was.

Stepping out of the bathroom, I turn toward where JD said he'll be waiting. As I'm passing by the main restrooms, I hear some girls talking through the door.

"Did you see that couple a few lanes down from us?"

"Oh my goodness, *yes*! The one with the blind girl, right?"

"Yeah. I think it's so sweet him bringing her here even though she can't see."

"I know. And damn, that guy is smokin' with a capital S. I'm kind of jealous. He's hot *and* seems really sweet. Where can I find one like that?"

"I know, right? She's really pretty too. Their baby is going to be gorgeous."

There are some scuffling sounds.

"Check out these highlights," one of them says, moving on from the topic of me and JD.

"Riley?" JD calls from down the hall.

I didn't realize I had stopped walking to listen to the girls. I head toward him, and he wraps an arm around my waist. I don't know how to feel about what the girls said. Maybe a little intimidated? What does an apparently 'smokin' hot' guy want with me? I know he mentioned wanting to get to know me, but why? *My* reasons are that I'm following my gut, but what are his?

They also mentioned the baby being *ours*. Although thinking of the baby as being ours sends shivers down my spine, I can't help but wonder why he would want to take on the role of being a father to my baby. Unless he's not planning on being around, and he's just wasting time for now. Maybe that's just how I should look at this for now as well. Just take each day as it comes with no expectations.

I'm distracted from my thoughts when I feel JD's thumb rub up and down where he's holding onto me. A skittering of goosebumps explodes over my skin, and I instinctively lean into him. We sit down side by side at the little table by our lane, and our food arrives shortly after.

"What do you look like?" I blurt out. "I mean, like, what color are your eyes? Your hair? That type of thing." I take a bite of my chicken fingers while I wait for his reply.

"Well, I have black hair and brown eyes."

When he doesn't elaborate, I chuckle, shaking my head. "Wow, I have the whole picture now."

I can hear him shifting a little in the chair beside me. I would actually love to feel him, feel his face, and get a picture of him that way. But I'm not sure how he'd react to that, especially here in public.

"I've never had to describe myself before."

I decide to let him off the hook for now. Maybe when we're in private, I'll ask to feel his face. I've noticed he's been touching me a lot more tonight; hands on my hips, around my waist, holding my hand, brief touches on my shoulder, but I've mostly kept my hands to myself so far. I think the doubts in my mind about him wanting to be with me have me holding back. He hasn't given me any indication that he's being anything other than genuine about wanting to hang out with me, and my instincts tell me there is something there between us. It's my head that's the problem.

"It's okay. You don't have to describe yourself." I offer a small smile. "Do you want to play another game after this?"

"Sure. Are you feeling okay?"

"Yep. I'm ready to kick your butt again."

I hear his soft chuckle as I take the last bite of my food.

By the time we make it back to my apartment, it's not late, but I'm still feeling tired. Pregnancy takes a lot out of me, and it doesn't take a lot to make me feel exhausted. Plus, I haven't been out having fun like this in a while.

"Thank you so much for tonight, JD. I really had a great time. And thank you so much for my headphones and the game. That was really sweet," I tell him as we approach my door. He offered to walk me here again, and I didn't hesitate to say yes.

"You're welcome. And I had a really good time tonight as well."

"Did you?" I find myself asking.

"Of course." The tone of his voice indicates that he doesn't know why I'd be asking that. This is one of those times where I wish I could see his face, his expressions. "I know you may not believe me, but I don't normally do this..." The strongest feeling of déjà vu washes over me, but he continues. "I don't usually date. Or talk much, for that matter. But there is something about you...I-I like you." He takes hold of my hand. "And if you're willing, I'd like to spend more time together."

I can feel the tears prickling at the back of my eyes at his sweet words but I somehow manage to hold them back. I take a deep breath and then pull my hand free from his, placing both of my hands on his chest instead.

I can both feel and hear the breath he sucks in upon contact.

I can feel the hardness of his muscular chest, but that's not what I'm interested in right now.

I feel the pounding of his heart against his ribcage as my hands pass by it and then continue sliding up to his shoulders.

Every inch my fingers climb, the more right it feels to be touching him. I can feel that he's wearing a button-up shirt, and the fact that he still felt it necessary to dress up for our date even though I can't see him touches my heart.

Once my hands reach his neck, I rest my head against his chest, slightly pulling him down at the same time to hug me back. His hands go around my body, and his cheek presses against my hair. No words are said for a few beats, but no words are needed.

Eventually, he pulls back, but instead of letting me go, his hands slide up to my cheeks, where he brushes his thumbs over my skin. "I'll see you at your appointment tomorrow, okay?"

I nod my head since my voice is lost in the feelings running through me. The next thing I feel is his soft lips pressed against mine in the gentlest kiss that lasts several seconds. JD doesn't try to deepen the kiss. He doesn't try to further anything, even though I think I'd let him if he did try.

He pulls back, rubs his thumbs along my cheeks once again, and then quietly says, "Goodnight, Riley."

"Goodnight," I whisper back.

CHAPTER THIRTEEN

Jasper

Are guys supposed to feel giddy? I'm not sure, but god, that's how I'm feeling right now with this excited buzz swimming through me. I've felt this way from the moment Riley let me touch my lips to hers, and I've barely been able to think of much else since.

As soon as I stopped thinking about Shay, stopped comparing the two, and focused on what was in front of me, focused on *Riley*, I realized how much I enjoyed *her* company.

I realized it was *Riley* who I liked.

It was *Riley*, who I liked touching.

And it wasn't at all just because she looked like Shay.

Last night I found that I kept making excuses for myself to be near her and touch her whenever I could. She looked so pretty, and her baby bump was so cute that I kept finding myself just staring at her throughout the night.

There's only one thing that bothers me with all of this, and it's the fact that I know that I don't want to be alone. I haven't since the day of my brother's funeral and the night with Shay. And for that reason, I just hope that I'm not latching onto her simply because I'd get an instant family out of it.

I like to think that that's not the case, though, because I'd like her regardless of whether she was pregnant or not.

Whenever she rubs her belly, I try not to think about how I wish her baby were mine, she'd probably freak out if she knew I was thinking that type of thing already. I know I'm getting ahead of myself and should slow down a little, but I find it hard with her. She's just so easy to be around, and I want everything with her already.

I offer a small smile to the couple that I just finished up with as they head out of the room. Knowing that I only have one more patient until Riley's appointment has my leg bouncing with anticipation. Thankfully, the time goes by quickly. When it's finally time to go out into the waiting room and call her name, I have to fight the urge to pull her straight into my arms. I move toward her with bright eyes and a smile on my face. She must know it's me standing in front of her because she looks up and smiles as well.

"Riley Brooks," I say quietly, placing my hand on hers.

"That's me," she replies just as quietly, then moves to stand up.

I continue holding her hand, loving the way it feels in mine. As we pass by the front receptionist's desk, Maya gives me a weird look, swinging her gaze between the two of us. I'm not quite sure what to make of her and her glare, but I'm too happy to care too much, so I ignore it and continue on.

I lead Riley into the room, and as soon as I close the door

behind us, my hands find her cheeks, and my mouth lands on hers. It's just a quick brushing of lips, but it feels fantastic to be able to do it nonetheless.

"Hi."

"Hi," she whispers back. "I almost convinced myself that yesterday didn't happen." My brows furrow, and I wait for her to elaborate on what she means. Reaching up, she latches on to both of my wrists. "It was the most fun I've had in a long while. It almost seemed surreal."

A smile crosses my face, and the touch of her hands wrapped around my wrists warms my skin. I bring my lips to hers again, telling her without words that it's the most fun I've had in a long while as well. I reluctantly pull back and then lead her over to the bed.

"How are you feeling today?" I ask once she's settled.

"Great, actually. I slept really well."

"Glad to hear it," I say softly. "May I?" I ask, holding the hem of her top. When she nods, I gently slide it up over her belly, my fingers brush over her skin along the way, and I see goosebumps form.

"And how are you, JD?" she asks when I sit back again.

I smile. "I'm great. Although, I didn't sleep as well as you. Too much on my mind, I guess."

"Bad things?"

"Good things."

Riley turns her head and smiles up at the ceiling. I get started on getting images and checking everything over with the new program. The baby is doing really well and looks perfect. A little nugget of guilt returns when I ask her again if she's sure she doesn't want to know the sex of the baby, and she tells me she doesn't. I really need to make sure I don't let it out accidentally.

Once I've gotten all of the images, I turn up the sound so that she can listen to the baby's heartbeat. I can't resist reaching for her hand as we sit there, listening to the fast little thumps through the speakers.

"So, did you get everything you needed for the new program?" she asks.

"Yes. I think it's going to work out well. It's more user-friendly."

"Hmm, well, too bad I don't have to come in again next week. I could have seen you again." She shakes her head and chuckles. "Well, not *seen* you, but you know what I mean."

"Can I have your number?" I blurt out. "I should have asked for it already by now instead of leaving it to chance as I did."

An odd look crosses her face, but then it's gone just as quickly. "Sure. You got some paper handy?"

"I have my phone," I say as I pull it out.

The relief I feel as I type in her numbers fills every part of me. I didn't realize just how much I needed it – a sure way to be able to contact her – even though I know where she lives now.

A several-month-long regret of not getting Shay's number tries to make its way to the surface, but I hold it down, forcing it to stay away. It doesn't matter that I don't have her's anyway, not now that I have Riley.

"Do you want to get lunch with me?" I ask, helping her stand up.

Regret fills her features as she faces me. "I'm sorry. I can't. I have to get to my sister's restaurant. I was supposed to work this morning, but I said I'd come in after my appointment instead."

Disappointment hits me like a brick. I'm already finding that I want to be around her all the time. "Oh, okay."

She smiles softly at me. "But I was planning on stopping by The Reading Nook later. Maybe I'll run into you there?"

"Okay."

Once we're all finished and she has her bag, I lead her to the bathroom. I intend to wait for her outside the door again, but Maya approaches and asks me to check something quickly.

"I'll be right back," I tell Riley before she closes the door.

"Sure."

I follow Maya to her desk, where she shows me some paperwork. It's just general stuff that didn't really need to be looked at and signed right now, but since I'm here anyway, I might as well do it.

"I didn't realize you had been seeing someone. And now you have a baby on the way? Wow."

I didn't realize I had been that obvious with Riley, but I guess Maya saw us at lunch together as well. "Actually, we only just started seeing each other," I answer as I sign.

"Oh? So it isn't your baby then?" she questions.

Her tone is surprised and somewhat judgmental, but when I look up at her, she only has a friendly smile on her face.

I hand her back the papers without answering her. "Here you go."

"Thanks, JD." She smiles again and walks away.

It took me a little longer than expected, so it doesn't surprise me when I get back and see that Riley is no longer in the bathroom. What *does* surprise me, though, is seeing her talking to Patrick further down the hallway.

"What's going on?" I can't help asking, and then I place my hand on Riley's lower back.

Patrick watches the movement, and I catch his eyebrows rising just the slightest bit. "Oh, nothing. I just wasn't watching where I was going and bumped into Riley here." He briefly touches her arm, and I don't like it, which is silly because I like Patrick. "Anyway, it was nice to meet you, Riley. Catch you later, JD."

I give him a nod and watch him as he walks away, curious about what they might have been talking about.

"Thanks for today," Riley says, drawing my attention back to her. "So, I'll see you tonight?"

I nod even though she can't see me, then say, "Yes. I'll be there."

She gives me a beautiful grin, and I feel my heart speed up again. I look up and down the hallway that we're standing in, and when I don't see anyone else around, I lean down and press my lips to hers again. I can't help it. Her mouth is addictive. I long to deepen the kiss, to delve into her mouth and get lost in her kisses, but I don't want to rush her, so I hold myself back again, settling for the few seconds of thrill I get, just barely touching her lips.

"I'll walk you out," I say when I pull back.

"Okay," she breathes out.

It's nice to know I'm having an effect on her as well, and it's not just one-sided. I take hold of her hand and lead her all the way to the front of the building, squeezing her hand before I say goodbye.

I expect her to get into a taxi or even an Uber, but instead, she continues walking down the street, using a cane to check the ground in front of her. I stay standing, watching her like a fool until she's almost at the end of the block.

Just as I go to finally turn away, I see a teenager step toward her and lightly kick at her cane. White-hot rage bubbles up within me, and I instantly break out into a sprint toward her. The kid's eyes widen when he sees me rushing at him, but he has no time to escape before I grab hold of his shirt and back him into the wall.

"What the hell do you think you're doing?!" I yell in his face.

"I–I."

"You what?! She's pregnant, for god's sake!"

The kid looks petrified, but I can't find it in me to feel bad for him. He was trying to hurt Riley. He was trying to hurt what's mine.

"I was just messin' with her."

"You think that makes it okay? That it's funny?" My grip tightens on his shirt.

"No! I know her, okay?" he says, looking over my shoulder. "I was just messin' with you, Riley."

I-what? I look back to see Riley standing there with wide eyes, and then recognition crosses her face.

"Matty?"

"Yeah," he says sheepishly. "I honestly wasn't tryin' to hurt you. I was just playin'."

My grip on his shirt loosens a little, but I'm still angry. "You could have hurt her."

I feel Riley touch me, and when she reaches my forearm, she grips it. "It's okay, JD. I know he's harmless."

After several seconds I sigh, my shoulders deflate, and I release the kid's shirt. He straightens himself out and then turns to Riley.

"I'm sorry, Riley. I really was just playin' around."

"It's alright. Now go on and get out of here and stop causing trouble. Oh, and say hi to your mom for me."

The kid gives a small smile and says, "I will." But when he looks back at me, the smile drops real quickly.

I watch as he runs off without looking back, and then I

turn back to Riley. "Are you okay?"

"Yes, JD. I'm totally fine. That was Matty, Sheryl's son. He really is harmless. Just likes to joke around a lot."

I nod as the anger starts to dissipate. "He still shouldn't have done it. I'll walk you to wherever you're headed."

"JD, *no*," she huffs out. I can see the frustration all over her face. "Just because I'm blind doesn't mean I can't walk myself. I'm quite capable–"

I cut her off with a finger to her lips. "It's not that. I know you're capable. But you have precious cargo." My hands land on her stomach, and her breath hitches. "When I saw someone trying to hurt you and the baby, or *thought* that's what was happening. I just...I haven't felt like that before."

Riley's features soften, and she moves in even closer to me. "Like what?" she whispers.

I go for honesty, trying to put my thoughts into words. "Like someone was mine to protect."

I don't see it coming, but in the next second, her hands slide up my chest to the back of my neck, and then she pulls my head down to crash into her lips. This is no soft peck but a passionate melding of our mouths. Her tongue parts my lips first, but I quickly take over, bringing my hands up to her cheeks and angling her head so I can deepen it.

A million sensations spark throughout my body as we kiss. A million fireflies light my insides. And a million fire-ants march through my veins. I can feel myself thicken in my pants as we kiss, so I try to slow it down and think of anything else that can help cool my body down.

The weather. Work. My parents. My brother.

In an instant, my dick settles, and I place one last kiss on her lips before resting my forehead on hers.

"You're still not walking me," she says, making me chuckle. "My sister's restaurant is only five blocks away."

I breathe in deeply through my nose, pulling her scent into my body like air. I nod against her head. "Okay."

"I'll see you tonight, alright?"

"Okay," I answer again and then straighten up.

She's wearing another one of her beautiful smiles on her face, and I already miss it before she's even turned around to continue walking.

CHAPTER FOURTEEN

Riley

"I'm sorry. I'm busy tonight," I say on the phone to my sister.

"Busy? Doing what?"

I resist the urge to sigh loudly. I know I haven't exactly had a super busy social life since the accident and finding out that I'm pregnant, but she always sounds like she can hardly believe that I have anyone other than her to hang out with.

"I'm going out with a friend."

JD feels like much more than a friend, but I'm not ready to tell Jordan about him just yet. I don't want her judgment or her worry. I don't want her to spoil it.

"A friend?"

"Yes. A friend. And they're going to be here any minute, so I've got to go."

I can tell she's dying to ask more, dying to pry into my life even further, but instead, she bites her tongue about it. "Okay, I'll see you tomorrow?"

"Yep. See you." I hang up before she can say anything else.

I feel like I've been floating all week. JD and I did meet up at The Reading Nook on Monday night and then again on Wednesday night. He continued to read to me even though he got me headphones. I have a suspicion that he secretly wants to find out what happens with the couple from the book.

Unfortunately for him, we reached an intimate moment in the book, and I could hear how uncomfortable he was reading it aloud to me. I have to give him credit, though, because he did not stop, regardless of how he might have felt. What I would give to see how flushed his cheeks probably were. I know he fidgeted a fair bit during that scene.

Unfortunately for *me*, listening to his voice as he described what was going on was a *huge* turn-on, and I could barely sit still myself.

We've texted a couple of times here and there since then, and tonight he's picking me up for another date. Apparently, we're going to an outdoor movie in the park where you bring blankets to sit on and your own food and drinks. I haven't watched a movie in a long time, but JD was right when he said that I could easily listen to one, especially one I've already seen.

Really though, I think I could easily do anything if it involved JD. He makes me feel special, and he makes me feel like I can still do a lot of things that I had given up on.

I decided to wear a dress that Jordan had bought for me last month. We have always had similar tastes in clothes, so

I trust her when she says it's cute and looks really good on me. It bunches up under my chest and then flows down to just above my knees.

My closet has been organized by Jordan in such a way that I can, to a certain extent, know what it is that I'm picking out. A sigh escapes me as I think about my sister. She really has done a lot for me. I should give her more of a break. It's just that she often makes me feel like I'm incapable of doing anything anymore, and I already have a problem with that.

I grab a pair of flats to wear and then walk back out to the living room just in time to hear a knock.

"Who is it?" I ask against the door.

"It's JD."

Smiling, I open the door. "Hi."

I feel one of his hands land on my cheek, followed by his lips on my mouth. "Hi, beautiful," he murmurs. "How're you both doing today?"

I notice his hand drop down to my stomach, and it causes my heart to leap inside my chest. Little gestures like this make me feel all gooey inside. "We're doing great." I try to keep my voice sounding as normal as possible.

I take a deep, steadying breath but then pause when I can smell something other than his cologne. He must notice me sniffing because he says, "It's the flowers I brought for you. I bought them for their fragrance. I figured you would think of me when you smelt them in your apartment."

Those gooey feelings come rushing back again. He places the flowers in my hand, and I take another deep breath, inhaling the fresh sweet aroma coming from them. I don't even need to know what type they are. They smell great.

"That is so sweet of you. Thank you, JD," I say. "Will you help me find something to put them in?"

"Sure."

JD steps inside, and I hear the click of the door as he closes it behind him and then follows me over to the kitchen.

"I think I still have a vase in one of the top kitchen cupboards." I see his black shadow move against my white kitchen cupboards, and then something occurs to me.

"Are you wearing black?" Now that I think about it, I think he's been wearing dark clothes every time I've seen him ever since I mentioned it to him.

"Yes. I thought it'd be easier for you to see me."

I chew on my bottom lip while trying to hold back my tears and the flood of emotions. He has been so incredibly thoughtful and always seems to go out of his way to do things for me.

I lay the flowers on the counter and then step closer to him, placing my hands on his shoulder to stop whatever he's doing. Once I know he's facing me, I slide my hands up to his cheeks and then bring his head down to capture his mouth with mine.

The moment our lips touch, a rush of lust courses through me. I love his taste, and I love his smell. My senses are heightened, and they respond to him like they can't get enough. I kiss him with all the adoration I feel for him in my heart.

Like before, I may have initiated it, but he takes over, parting my lips to sweep his tongue into my mouth. His arms come around my back to hold me as close as possible without squishing my belly.

He deepens the kiss, and our tongues move together in a sensual dance, so naturally. As if they've done it a thousand times before. Eventually, he pulls away just slightly and rests his forehead against mine. Our breaths mingle together in the space between us.

Instead of letting his cheeks go, I start trailing my fingers over his face, feeling along his strong jawline first, then to the slightest dip in his chin. After that, I trace up to his soft lips that kiss my fingertips as they pass over them. Next, I feel along his straight nose, over his eyes, feeling the flutter of his long lashes, and then along his eyebrows.

I continue feeling over his face, painting a picture of him in my head. My imagination puts together a handsome man. But at this point, it wouldn't matter what he looked like because of the way he makes me feel and his beautiful personality.

Once I've gotten enough of a picture of him, my hands make their way up to his hair, and I run my fingers through the silky strands. He lets out a humming sound that makes me smile.

"I like it when your fingers touch me," he whispers.

"I like it too." I would love to continue the journey to the rest of his body as well, but we need to get going soon, so I'll settle for this right now.

He kisses me one more time, then, after a swallow that is loud enough for me to hear, he clears his throat and stands up straighter. "I found a vase. I'll just put the flowers in, and then we can go."

"Okay." I smile.

When we arrive at the park, he opens my door, grabs my hand, and pulls me to my feet. I hear him open the trunk and get something out, and then we're walking. Cheerful chatter can be heard as we go, but I can't tell how many people there are and can't make out anything else around us except for a big bright rectangle which I'm guessing is the screen.

We come to a stop, and JD tells me to stay standing for a moment. I listen to the sound of his movements, the sounds of a blanket being shaken open, and other various noises.

After a minute, he takes my hand again.

"Okay, take a step, and then you can lower yourself onto the blanket." I do as he says and sit down on the soft blanket he spread out for us. "I brought some pillows to lean on to make it more comfortable for you as well."

"JD," I say, shaking my head. "This is so lovely, thank you."

He leans in and presses a quick kiss to my lips. I've noticed he usually places a hand on my jaw before he kisses me. It's kind of like a heads-up that it's about to happen since I can't really see it coming.

"We have about twenty minutes until the movie starts. I brought sandwiches for an easy dinner and some snacks for the movie. Do you want to eat now?"

"Yes, please."

"I read that pregnant women should avoid deli meats, so I made roasted chicken BLTs."

The tone of his voice suggests that he's unsure of how I would take the fact that he's been looking up information on pregnant women. All I can think, though, is how incredibly easy it is to fall in love with him, especially since he keeps doing such sweet and thoughtful things for me.

"That sounds great." I smile.

"Would you like a bottle of water or apple juice?"

"Apple juice, please."

He hands me the sandwich and juice, and we both quietly eat, listening to the chatter around us. Once we're finished, he arranges the pillows and then leans back, pulling me to lay on his shoulder. My belly is kind of leaning against him, and his arm holds me close.

It almost feels like we've been together for a long time already, and this is something that we often do. The only reason it *doesn't* feel like that is that my stomach is filled with butterflies and excitement at being this close to him, lying down with him for the first time.

The people surrounding us on their own blankets and chairs quiet down as the movie starts. The familiar opening scene of Fred Savage playing a video game in bed while he's sick fills the speakers in the park. I've seen The Princess Bride so many times that I can picture it easily. This was such a good idea, and I'm so glad JD brought me.

"Are you comfortable?"

"Mhmm," I answer, snuggling in a little closer.

I feel him kiss the top of my head, and I just about melt right here on the ground. I always love it when the guy in a book I'm reading does that. It's like an intimate gesture of affection mixed with protectiveness. Like he just needed to have that little bit of connection and couldn't help himself.

At some point during the movie, JD pulls out some snacks and places them on his stomach for us both to reach easily. A couple of times, I pretended to miss the containers and purposely touched his stomach instead. I've enjoyed the reaction I've gotten out of him each time. Either a twitch of his muscles, sucking in a sharp breath, or simply just a little shift of his body. I can't help but wonder if he enjoys the touch.

In different parts of the movie, when there isn't any talking, he quietly narrates in my ear what is happening in the scene. He is seriously the sweetest man. I mean, who does this?

By the end of the movie, even though I didn't see a thing, it feels like I watched the whole movie. I push myself up and feel for JD's face. When I get to his cheek, I gently rub my thumb over his skin.

"Thank you so much for this. I feel like I'm always thanking you. But I mean it. You're amazing."

He grabs my hand and kisses my palm and then my fingers. "I think you're the amazing one."

I lean down, thankfully hitting the right target with my lips. I kiss him slowly, learning the feel of his lips, the taste of his mouth, and the caress of his tongue. All the while, his hands rub up and down my back. I could easily lose myself in him right here and now. If it weren't for the sounds of the people around us, I could pretend we're here alone, that no one else exists.

Reluctantly, I pull away. "Where did you come from?" I whisper.

"I've been right here, waiting for you." Before I can respond, some music starts playing. "C'mon, it's time to dance."

"What?" I question as he gets up and pulls me to my feet as well.

"This is a movie and a dance night."

"Are you serious?" I laugh.

"Very." He places my hands on his shoulders and wraps his around my back, holding me close as we begin to sway.

I close my eyes and lay my head on his chest. I can feel his heart beating against my cheek, and the scent of his cologne surrounds me. I can't believe how quickly I'm falling for him. Then again, with Jasper, I was almost there after only one night. Maybe it just happens easily for me.

JD rests his cheek on the top of my head, and I let out a sigh. "One more thing ticked off your list," he murmurs.

I chuckle softly. "I'll have to think of more things to put on it."

"I look forward to hearing what else you think you can't do just so that I can prove you wrong."

A drip of water hits my cheek, and at first, I think it's a

tear from JD, but then another one hits, and then one on my arm.

"It's starting to rain. The clouds came over quickly. Come on. I'll take you to my car and then come back for the stuff."

"No. No, it's okay. I want to stay in it."

"You do?" I can hear the uncertainty in his voice. But I'm high on life right now from the wonderful night and this wonderful man.

I nod. The weather is still warm, so the drops feel refreshing. I can hear the people around us hustling to pack up their stuff and make it to cover before they get soaked. Squealing and laughing as they go. But I stay where I am.

The rain starts getting heavier, drowning out every other sound. I open my arms wide, facing the sky, and just enjoy it pounding into my flesh.

"Feel it hitting your skin, JD. Smell it in the air. Live in the moment. Just *feel*."

After a few minutes, there is only the sound of the rain. The other people are gone, and it suddenly occurs to me that I'm not sure where JD is. I drop my arms to my side. He didn't reply to me before. It's dark, and I don't have my cane. My heartbeat quickens as a minuscule amount of panic begins to grow. As much as I want my independence, I know I would have no idea how to leave this place if I were alone right now. I hate this feeling of being scared and helpless.

"JD?" I can't help the panic in my voice. "JD, where are you?"

"I'm right here," he says close behind me, and then I feel his hands land on my hips. "I was just watching you." This time his voice is close to my ear.

Relief rushes through me, my heart settles down, and I lean my head back on his chest. He slides his hands up along my sides until he reaches my shoulders and gives a squeeze, then he continues down my arms, down to my hands, and then threads his fingers through mine. Bringing our joined hands up, he holds them out to the sides as I had them moments ago. His body behind me brings so much comfort and warmth.

I'm not sure how long we stand there in the rain together, but we're both completely soaked by the time he turns me around and hugs me close.

"Thank you," he whispers.

"For what?"

"For giving me a chance. For letting me into your world."

I smile while my heart expands to twice its size in my chest. "Are you busy tomorrow night?"

"No." His hand rubs circles on my back.

"I think I'd really like to try those taco wraps you told me about."

CHAPTER FIFTEEN

Riley

"I'm kind of jealous of your eyebrows," Jordan says from in front of my face.

"I think you've told me that a time or two before."

"Well, it's true. I'm reminded of it every time you ask me to tidy them up, and I see there's practically nothing to do." I chuckle at her. "Why did you ask me to do it right now, anyway? This storage room doesn't exactly have the best lighting."

"I just realized that I hadn't had you check them for a few weeks, and the storage room was the only place I could finally corner you."

"Mhmm, so you stop me working to do it right now?"

I picture her standing there with her arms crossed and her hip sticking out. She knows something is up. I had planned on telling her anyway, seeing as JD is going to be here shortly to pick me up. I figured it would be good to introduce her to him so she would feel a little better about me dating him. She can see for herself how nice he is.

I take in a deep breath. "Okay, the thing is, I have a date tonight."

"What?"

"Remember Sheryl said I was with a guy at her cafe?"

"Yes," she says, slowly drawing out the word. "The guy who did your ultrasound and then randomly asked you out."

I roll my eyes. "It wasn't like that." Well, it kind of was, I guess, but whatever. "I've actually spent some more time with him, and we've... been on a few dates."

"What? When?"

"It doesn't matter," I tell her, standing up from the crate I was sitting on. "The point is, I like him, and we're seeing each other."

She's quiet for a moment, and I can practically hear the skepticism oozing out of her. "Okay," she finally says.

"Okay?"

"Yeah. Okay."

I place my hands on my hips. "No, 'I don't like this, Riley'. Or 'He's probably a murderer'. Or 'He just wants to steal your baby?'"

"Geez, give me a break. I don't sound like that."

"You usually kinda do."

She comes and places an arm around my shoulders and sighs. "You're a grown woman, Riley, and I have to trust that you know what you're doing."

"Wow. That's... are you sure you're feeling okay?"

She punches my arm lightly and laughs. "Shut up. Troy

told me to lighten up a little with you, so I'm trying to be better, alright?"

"Well, that's good to hear. I'll have to thank Troy. And the reason I wanted you to check my eyebrows right *now* is that he's picking me up from here. I'm going to his place tonight."

"From here? I guess you're pretty serious about him if you're having him meet me."

"Well, it's not like we're getting married right away. But yeah. I do really like him, and I'm serious about dating him."

I feel her arms encircle me with a quick hug. "Then I'm happy for you." Her arms drop down, and she pulls on my hands. "Now, when will he be here 'cause I gotta make sure he's not a murderer."

Our laughter mixes together as we make our way out of the storage room.

"Did you even get what you were supposed to get out of there?" I ask.

"No. I'll just send Amy back in there in a minute instead. I want to wait at the entrance with you. Tell me what he's supposed to look like."

I laugh again as she leads me easily with her arm threaded through mine through the tables to the desk at the front. I admit I'm pretty curious as to what she'll think of his looks. Not that it would change things for me.

"He told me he has black hair and brown eyes. And I think that he's maybe about a head taller than me. Probably not quite that much. I'd say my head reaches his chin."

We stop at the front, where my sister proceeds to watch through the window for anybody that matches the description I gave.

"Hmm, nope, that guy is blond... That one has his arm around somebody else.."

"What are you doing?" Melody, another girl that usually works the front desk with me, asks.

"Keep an eye out for someone with black hair and brown eyes," Jordan tells her. "A guy."

"Oooh. Okay! Let me see...Ginger, gray, black hair, but he looks fourteen."

I laugh and shake my head. "How about you just wait for him to walk in?"

"No way," Jordan protests. "We'll be able to check him out properly without him seeing us. If he looks all scowly and rude before he enters, then he's probably no good."

Somehow I can't imagine him ever acting that way. My heart beats wildly inside my chest in anticipation. I'm both excited and nervous to see what the girls think of him, especially Jordan, since she's the closest thing to a mother figure that I have.

"Okay, I see black hair, tall, fit. Can't see his eye color... but wow," Melody says.

"Wow, is right. Sis, if that guy is him, then I am thoroughly impressed."

"Right, because–"

"Nope. Don't go there," Jordan chastises. "I would be impressed regardless, okay?"

"Which way is he headed?" Melody says more so to herself.

"Oh, it looks like he's definitely coming this way." Jordan grips my arm. "He has a soft, sweet smile on his face, but he doesn't look like a pussy."

"Aww, he's holding the door open for that couple to come in here first. Such a gentleman," Melody whisper-shouts.

"Oh my goodness. I definitely think it's him. He just got a big smile on his face when he saw you," Jordan mumbles in my ear. "He actually looks a little familiar. Maybe I've seen him around before. Okay, shhh, he's coming."

I chuckle. "I've barely said a word."

I can see the shadow approach us, and then a hand lands on the opposite hip of where Jordan is standing. "Hi, Riley." A second later, his lips land on my cheek, and his cologne fills my nose. I love it so much that I almost find myself sniffing at him before he moves back.

"Hey." I can feel my cheeks warming as a blush crawls its way up from my neck. "JD, this is my sister Jordan. And Melody works here with me."

"Nice to meet you," he says politely.

"Nice to meet you, too," Melody responds.

"Likewise," Jordan says, squeezing my arm again. I think she's telling me she likes him, but I can't be sure. "So, you're an ultrasound technician?"

"That's right."

"That's interesting. I don't think I've met a male one before."

"I hear that a lot." I can tell that he's in his default – not talking a whole lot – mode, and it actually makes me feel special that he's able to converse normally with me.

"So, Riley tells me you guys are heading to your place?"

"Yes. I'll be cooking us dinner," JD says in his smooth, sexy voice. I'm pretty sure I just heard the girls swoon at the fact that he's cooking dinner.

"That's so nice. But no offense, can I get your address?" And there's the Jordan I know.

"Of course, none taken."

He rattles off his address, and Jordan lets go of my arm. I'm pretty sure she's writing it down so that if anything happens, she can send the cops there. I do appreciate that she's being safe, but I know I don't need it.

A big hand takes hold of mine, and then JD asks, "Are you ready to leave, or do you still have some things to do?"

"No, I'm ready to go," I say and turn in the direction that I'm sure Jordan and Melody are. "Bye, girls."

"Have a good night, ladies," JD says to them.

"Hold up." I feel Jordan's arms come around me for a hug. "You did good," she whispers in my ear. "He's super hot and seems sweet. Have fun. Love you. Oh, and text me later or tomorrow."

I have weird, mixed feelings about the fact that she likes him. On the one hand, I'm so happy that she approves and thinks I've done well and have found a great guy. But on the other hand, I still have those lingering thoughts and wonder why he would would want me. Because really, I'm not that great a catch.

"Thanks. I will," I whisper back.

JD holds my hand all the way to his car, letting me know along the way when there is uneven ground or a step. I let him do it instead of using my cane because I know that he's not doing it simply because he thinks I'm incapable but rather because it makes him feel good. He said the other day that he felt like I was his to protect.

I'm stopped by his hand on my shoulder just as I'm about to get into his car. One of his hands grips the back of my neck while the other one lifts my jaw so that our lips can easily connect.

His tongue parts my lips and dives straight in to meet mine. He tastes of mint, and his scent fills my lungs, making me feel lightheaded and causing a warmth to spread between my legs. His kisses are passionate, and our mouths move together in a carefully orchestrated dance. The result is me panting and wanting more.

All too quickly, he pulls back, and I wish we were already

alone so that I could dive back into his arms and kiss him all over.

"I wanted to do that when I first saw you. But even though I haven't met a woman's family before, I didn't think it would be considered appropriate."

I laugh softly as he caresses my cheek with his thumb. "You've never met a girlfriend's parents?" I try to keep the delight out of my voice.

"No. I haven't really had a girlfriend before."

I know he said he doesn't usually date, but I had figured there was at least someone special at some point. It surprises me since he's such an attentive, caring man. It's yet another reason for me to feel special.

CHAPTER SIXTEEN

Riley

There's a fresh scent that hits my nose the second I walk through the door to JD's townhouse. It's a mixture of clean laundry, cleaning products, and a vanilla-scented candle. There's also a masculine smell mixed in with all of it, Jasper's scent, making it all the more alluring. I love it. Besides the fact that I'm pregnant, and that generally gives you a heightened sense of smell, being blind has heightened all of my other senses as well.

JD leads me around his home, describing what's around me and the direction of where things are, giving me a clear picture.

"There is nothing on the floor that will trip you, so if you want to explore a little yourself, you can."

"Maybe later. Can I help with dinner? I know there isn't

really a lot that I can do, but I'd like to do something."

"There is plenty you can do." He wraps an arm around my waist. "Come on. You can cut the cucumbers."

"Cut?" I question, a little unsure.

"Yes."

Standing behind me with his hands on mine, JD guides the knife down through the vegetable. He's pressed lightly against my back, and his breath tickles my neck as he speaks.

"Just keep your fingers folded inwards like that, and you won't cut them. Go slow."

He repeats the slicing motion a few more times until he thinks I have the hang of it and then steps away. I can sense that he's still close by, keeping an eye on what I'm doing. It puts me at ease. I carefully continue to cut, not sure if it's straight or not, but just the fact that I'm cutting food again has me feeling pretty damn thrilled.

"I know this is just something simple, but being able to do this again..." I shake my head. "It's pretty amazing."

I feel a kiss on the side of my head. "Just like you."

If I weren't actually pretty hungry and looking forward to eating these taco wraps, then I would probably just forget about the food, turn to JD, and try to make him feel as good as he always makes me feel. But as it is, this baby wants to be fed first. So, I continue to help with cutting a few more things, and then JD gets me to stir the meat. It smells so good in here that my mouth waters.

"Okay. You take a seat here, and I'll bring everything to the table," JD says after pulling a chair out at the table and leading me to it.

Once everything is brought over, and I have the wrap in my hands ready to eat, I pause with it halfway to my mouth, feeling hesitant again.

JD must sense my apprehension because he says, "Riley, I don't care if you make a mess."

I smile, immediately feeling at ease. "Well, you might when you go to kiss me later, and I have food on my face."

He chuckles from across the table, making my smile grow. When I take my first bite, I groan out loud. It's *so* good. I had deprived myself of tacos since not being able to see, and even though these are wraps, they still have the taco flavoring, and there is crunch from the taco shells inside. My sense of taste is definitely off the charts right now.

"I'm glad you approve," JD says.

We don't talk much while we eat, but it doesn't matter. Even with the silence, just his presence near me is enough to fill any emptiness which I would have had at my place all alone.

"Guess what I brought?" I ask once I've helped him clean up and fill the dishwasher.

"What?"

I locate my bag and put my hand inside to find what I'm looking for. When I feel it, I pull it out. "This. The tic-tac-toe you gave me." I smile. "Maybe you'll be better at it than bowling?"

"Considering I haven't played it before, I'm not so sure."

"What! How could you not have played it before?" I ask incredulously. "It sounds like you never did anything fun while growing up."

He's silent for a moment, and it occurs to me that maybe that sounded a bit rude.

"Not really. I was...sheltered. I guess you could say."

"Oh, I'm sorry."

I remember Jasper talking a little about his parents and how they never let him do anything, either. Is that a thing?

Super strict parents producing kind, sweet men? No, that can't be so. I knew guys in high school who had kind of strict parents, and they went totally wild. Some were assholes too. It's just simply a coincidence.

"Don't be. And don't worry, I plan on kicking your butt."

I grin, shifting a little closer to him on the couch. "Is that right?"

"Yes."

I move even closer to him so that our thighs are now pressed together, and I can feel the heat radiating from his body. Suddenly, I'm not thinking about playing the game anymore. Suddenly, all I can think about doing is touching him all over. It's what I've been wanting to do for a little while now. The air around us changes. Does he want this as well? I'm somewhat nervous, but I need to ask this now. I don't want to wait any longer.

"Actually, JD, can I feel you?" I swallow. "I mean, *all* of you."

I feel him shift a little. "Yes," he whispers.

I turn myself so that I'm facing him better and then tentatively reach for him. My hands slide up his arm first. I've felt his arm before, but this is different. I glide over his muscles and trace over every vein. There's not a groove I've left untouched by the time I reach his shoulder.

He lets out a shuddered breath as I continue moving along to his neck and jaw. When I reach the top button of his short-sleeve button-down shirt, I pause for a second, hoping we're on the same page.

His hand lands on my thigh and begins moving back and forth, giving me confirmation to go ahead. I continue moving down his shirt, unbuttoning each button as quickly as possible. Once they're all undone, I open it up and splay my hands across his warm skin.

Feeling over his abs first, I consider including my tongue on my travels but decide against it. Instead, I continue exploring all over his torso with my hands only. My thumbs brush over his nipples as they pass by, and he sucks in a breath. I'll have to remember that for later.

My hands feel greedy, not wanting to stop touching him at all. I make several passes over his upper body before I stop at the button of his pants. His hand that was gently caressing my leg at first is now pressing a lot harder into my flesh and has moved higher on my thigh. I'm so turned on right now, and we've barely even touched each other. There's something so sensual about doing all of this without saying any words. He's letting me explore him the way I want, with my hands, and nothing else is needed yet.

When he gives my leg a squeeze as if he's giving me permission to continue, I start undoing his pants. I can feel his erection pressing against his zipper as I work on sliding it down. I love that I'm making that happen. I love that I'm turning him on despite everything. It makes my own desire increase even more.

He lifts his hips and pushes his pants down along with his boxer briefs. I avoid his dick for now and move to sit on the floor in front of him. I start at his feet, discovering that they're ticklish, and then continue up his legs.

His breathing is getting louder now, and it spurs me on. He has a gorgeous body. Muscly but not too bulky. Besides the hair on his legs, a little on his chest, and a happy trail, his skin is so smooth to the touch. I trail my hands up and down his legs a few times, admiring the muscles in his thighs that tense up when I slide my hands over them.

Finally, *finally*, I reach for his dick. The skin is velvety smooth and hot under my fingers. One hand cups his balls while the other makes slow strokes of his shaft. He lets out a low groan, bringing a pleased smile to my face. I lick my lips and tighten my grip on him, but not even a few seconds later, I'm abruptly picked up, causing a little yelp to escape me.

JD settles me onto his lap so that I'm straddling him, and then his hands cup my cheeks right before his lips crash into mine. I let out a moan as he kisses me deeply and desperately, like he'll die if he doesn't get a taste right now.

My hands thread through his hair, tugging at the roots, which pulls another groan from him that rumbles from his chest. His hands leave my face to travel over my body. Only his movements aren't done with as much finesse. They're all over the place, like he doesn't know what he wants to touch first. Or he wants to touch everything all at once and doesn't have enough hands.

He wrenches his mouth away from me, breathing heavily. "Is this okay?"

"More than okay." I pull his lips back to mine, and he kisses me back with as much passion as I feel.

Our mouths move together as we try to pull each other closer. I rock back and forth over his bare length. I'm still dressed while he's naked. I've read a lot of books where it's the opposite. The guy is fully dressed in a suit or something, and the woman is completely naked. It seems to make the guy feel powerful.

That's not the case here. I want my clothes to be stripped off so that I can feel his skin against mine. So that I can feel every movement of his muscles against my body while he moves over me and claims me. His lips move to my neck, and I automatically bend it to allow him better access.

"If you want to stop this at any point, just tell me," he says against my skin. I nod, even though there is no chance that I'll be stopping it. "Hold onto me." It's the only warning he gives before gripping my ass and standing up.

While he walks us to probably his bedroom, I lean in to take a deep breath against his neck and slip my tongue out to taste his skin. His fingers tighten on my ass in response, so I do it again.

"I'm laying you back on my bed now," he says and then lowers me down. "Remember, we can stop this at any point."

"JD?"

"Yes?"

"Undress me already."

"Thank goodness." He wastes no time complying, undressing me in record time.

My nipples pucker once I'm fully naked on his bed. I'm propped up on some pillows, leaning against his headboard. I don't know where he's looking or even what my body looks like at this moment.

"Do you know how beautiful you are? How sexy?" he asks. "My turn to touch *you* now."

I feel each of his hands on my ankles. They glide up my legs, continuing all the way to the tops of my thighs and then back down again. He repeats it a few times. Similar to what I did to him. Goosebumps form under his touch, and I start squirming with need. I need to feel him close to me.

His hands don't stop at my thighs this time; they continue up over my belly and onto my breasts. He squeezes them and rubs over my sensitive nipples before I feel the wetness of his mouth, licking and sucking over each one. A gasp of pleasure comes from my mouth before he swallows it down with another kiss. One of his hands remains playing with my nipples while the other explores the area between my legs.

As much as I enjoy what he's doing to me, I don't want to wait much longer. I need him closer. I reach for him, pulling and gripping him to me. His mouth leaves mine to taste my neck and jaw first, and then he showers kisses all over my face. Every touch from him has a heightened response in my body since I'm unable to see what he's doing.

I slide my hands down his back, loving the feel of his muscles flexing as he moves. Then I move my hands around between us, searching until I reach his thick erection, gripping it in my fist. He lets out a hiss as I rub it over myself.

"Are you clean, JD?" I ask against his lips.

"Yes."

"I'm clean, too." I guide him to my opening, ready to connect our bodies, but he doesn't push in yet.

"Are you sure?" he asks again.

"JD, I'm more sure about this than anything el–"

Before I can even finish the sentence, he thrusts into me. Delicious sensations hum through my veins at the feel of him inside me, with nothing between us. Flesh touching flesh. Skin touching skin.

His erratic breathing heats my neck as he holds himself above me, unmoving. I reach up, tugging gently at his hair so that I can turn his head and kiss his lips. When our lips touch, he starts moving, gliding in and out.

He holds a steady pace at first while kissing all over my face. Every now and then, he whispers to me how good it feels and how beautiful I am.

With each thrust he makes, pleasure sparks within me. His hips swivel in such a way that his dick strokes the perfect spot inside me. I'm beginning to fall apart beneath him, and I don't want to be held together.

I've felt this all-consuming feeling once before, but this seems to be even better. It's probably because there are so many more feelings involved this time. I'm falling hard and fast for JD. Maybe I'm already in love with him. He doesn't see me as helpless. He doesn't seem to mind that

I'm pregnant already. And for the briefest moment, I wish this baby were his. That's the last thought before the most intense orgasm floods through my body, and I lose all sense of time. My mind blanks, and I tremble.

"JD," I barely breathe out.

I don't know if it was more intense because of my sight being gone or because of the feelings involved, but either way, I'm gone for this man. He grips my hair in a sexy, possessive move, and we kiss again. His movements become faster and uncontrolled. Both of us lost in the swirl of feelings surrounding us.

JD moves so that his knees are bent under my thighs and pounds into me even harder. I'm vaguely aware of him shuddering above me shortly afterward and his warmth filling my insides. It causes another, less intense orgasm to flow through me, but it's in no way less satisfying.

I can't help but let a goofy smile take over my face as I lay completely boneless and sated.

CHAPTER SEVENTEEN

Jasper

I collapse my upper body to the side of Riley so that I don't crush her, but I'm still buried deep inside her, and I kind of want to stay there forever. We're both breathing heavily, and I can't seem to catch my breath.

That was more than just intense. That was... well, fuck, no words can describe it. Does she know what she does to me? I feel the urge to tell her that I love her over and over. I want to make love to her over and over. I want to hold her and never let her go. I want to tell her that I'll look after her and the baby forever.

But I don't want to scare her off, so I don't say any of it. I think that I most likely need her love and affection more than she needs mine. Now that I've had a taste of what it's like, I don't think I could live without it. I know that she feels *something* for me, but that doesn't necessarily mean that she's ready to hear me declare my love for her. I know this has all happened fast, even for me.

She tenses suddenly and presses on her belly with a grimace. I quickly pull out and sit up beside her. Dread fills my gut, thinking I've somehow caused her pain.

"Are you okay? What's wrong? Did I hurt you?"

"Relax." She lets out a breathy chuckle. "It's just a cramp. I've read about it in my pregnancy books. They're pretty common after an orgasm. Especially after a really good one."

"Yeah?" I can't hide the pride in my voice. Knowing that *I* gave her that really good orgasm is an ego boost.

She grins. "Yeah."

My heart begins to settle down now that I know she's okay. I place my hand over the top of hers and begin moving them in circles, rubbing over where her cramp was. I watch our hands moving together and then eventually slide mine off of hers so that I'm rubbing directly on her stomach. Her skin is so soft. I continue moving gently in small circles until I feel movement under my hand and then freeze.

"Did you feel that?" Riley asks.

"Yes."

There are more movements under my hand, and I press a little harder to feel it better. I've seen babies move on the screen at work, and in the pregnancies that are further along, I've seen a foot or a hand poking out. There's even sometimes movement under the transducer. But this is the first time I've felt a baby move under my hand, and I'm in awe. It makes the fact that there is actually a little human in there all the more real.

When I look back up at Riley to see if she's as excited about it as I am, her eyes are closed. I figure she must be exhausted. "I'll bring something to clean you up, don't move."

I return to her with a wet washcloth and start cleaning between her legs while she looks in my direction with sleepy eyes. It's as if she can see me, see my every move, but I know she can't. I would be happy to do this for her every day. I want her to be mine.

Once she's cleaned up, she yawns. "I still need to go to the bathroom, you know."

I kiss her sleepy smile and grab her hand. "Come on, then."

I guide her to the bathroom, letting her know where things are, and then go back to the bed to pull the blankets back and slip in. If she wants me to help her back, I will. Otherwise, I'll wait here for her.

A couple of minutes later, she comes out of the bathroom and slowly walks in the direction of my bed. I've noticed she has a good sense of direction. I'm not sure if it's something she has developed since becoming visually impaired or if she's always been good with it.

"About five more steps," I say.

She reaches the end and proceeds to crawl up the bed. She's still naked, and the beautiful vision of her on all fours crawling toward me has my dick going hard again. I ignore it, though, and pull her to me, positioning her back to my front and holding her close.

"Stay the night?" I mumble in her ear. We hadn't exactly planned it, but I'm hoping it was a given.

"Okay."

I swallow thickly, thinking about the last time I slept the night with someone. "Will you be here when I wake up?"

"Do you want me to be?"

"Yes."

She places her hand on top of mine that is sitting on her stomach, then threads her fingers through mine. "Then, I will be."

I breathe out a sigh of relief and lean down to kiss her cheek. This feels so right, so comfortable, and it doesn't take long for me to fall asleep.

***

Lick, suck, stroke.

My mind begins to stir. I'm somewhere in the space between deep sleep and wakefulness, where awareness is just starting to trickle in. Riley. I remember our perfect night together. Sinking into her for the first time. Falling asleep, holding her.

Wet, warmth, swirl.

I remember waking through the night and taking her from behind. Both of us were barely conscious but still knew exactly what we were doing. The memories seem to be accompanied by the feelings as well. Or is this just a really good half-awake dream?

The sucking sensation gets stronger, and my eyes pop open. That's not a dream or my imagination. I look down to see Riley's head bobbing up and down. *Shit*, that feels good.

"Riley," I barely choke out through the pleasure. "You don't have to do that."

She hums, heightening the already intense feelings before releasing me with a pop. "I *want* to."

She takes me in her mouth again, not waiting for a reply. *Fuck.* I gather her hair in my hand and hold it out of the way. I'm unable to stop myself from pumping upwards into her mouth. It feels too good. She seems to love it as well and makes more humming noises. All I can do is watch in fascination as she brings me closer to the edge and then pushes me right over.

I groan out my orgasm, squeezing my eyes shut, praising Riley over and over. After swallowing down every last drop that I give her, she finally releases me. My dick twitches, and a few tremors shake through my body at the same time. That's certainly a good way to wake up in the morning.

I let out a contented sigh. "Shit. That was nice."

"*Nice?*"

"*Really* nice."

Her laugh is like sweet music to my ears. "I'm glad it's another thing I can still do," she says and settles into my side.

"Mhmm, you can. Whenever you like."

She giggles again, and I join her with my own chuckle. I would love to wake up like this every day. I'm not even talking about the blow job thing – although I wouldn't be opposed to it – I mean having her in my bed, talking and laughing with her, holding her.

"I should feed you now and then return the favor," I say, kissing her head.

"Mm. Yeah, the baby is hungry," she says with a smile. "I kind of am too."

"I thought so. Okay, how about some eggs, bacon, and pancakes? Sound good?"

"Sounds perfect," she mumbles.

"Alright, you can stay here if you like."

"No. I'll come and keep you company."

I kiss her again. "Okay." Then I find her clothes from last night for her to put on and get myself dressed.

"So, what's the most embarrassing thing you did when you were younger?" she asks while I'm pulling out all the food.

"That's pretty random." I chuckle. I have to think for a moment because it's not like I really did anything out of the ordinary. My life as a child was, in one word, boring. "There is one thing, but it's not really something that I did, but rather, something that happened to me."

"Okay." Riley sits forward, resting her elbows on the counter, eager for me to continue.

"In junior high, I sat between this girl and guy, Casey and Eric. I didn't really know them well. Anyway, this one day, he was leaning forward, trying to get her attention, but she was too busy taking notes or something. I saw that he had a note in his hand and offered to give it to her. The teacher looked at me right when I was about to pass it to her."

"Oh, no." Riley puts her hands over her mouth. "I can see where this is going."

"The teacher told me that I had to stand up and read it out loud to the class. It was filled with all of these crude descriptions of what he wanted to do to Casey. Everyone assumed I had written it, even her. And Eric never admitted that it was his. My face was so red."

"Oh, god." Riley tries to hold back a laugh but is unsuccessful. A hearty chuckle fills the air. "I'm so sorry for laughing," she says, wiping tears away.

I start chuckling as well. "It was so embarrassing at the time, and it took a while to get over because people kept talking about it, and the girl switched seats. But it's kind of funny now."

"I love it." She grins.

We chat some more while I cook and then sit down at the table to eat. Everything about this feels natural, even though I haven't had a woman stay here before. I practically stare at her beautiful face the entire time we eat. I'm kind of grateful that she can't see my obsessed-like behavior. I'm sure if she could see my eyes, she'd know. She'd see how far gone I am for her.

"Oh my goodness!" Riley says, placing her hands over her face after I take her empty plate away. "I just realized that I don't even know your last name. I feel like I know so many other random things about you. And then I slept with you before I even thought to ask."

She shakes her head and then drops her hands to her stomach, rubbing over it. I chuckle a little. It hadn't even occurred to me either, probably because I already knew her last name.

"It's DeLarouge."

"Okay." She nods. "JD DeLarouge."

"Actually, no, JD is my initials." Now I do actually feel bad because I'm so used to people calling me that, that I never thought to tell her otherwise.

"Oh?"

"I'm sorry, everyone just calls me that because it's easier, so I usually go by that. My name is Jasper DeLarouge." I start filling the sink with water to wash the few dishes instead of putting them in the dishwasher.

"It's Jasper? Your name is Jasper?"

"Yes." It's nice hearing my name come from her lips. I should have told her right at the beginning.

"Would you like some more juice or water?" When she doesn't answer me, I turn around. Her chin is dipped, facing the table. Her brows are bunched together, and her face looks pale. "Are you okay?" I ask, drying my hands and making my way over to where she is.

"Um, yeah." She blinks fast a few times. "Actually, no. My stomach is suddenly not feeling so good."

"Do you want to go lay down on my bed?"

She swallows. "I think I'd like to be in my own bed."

"Oh, okay." I can't help but feel disappointed that she

doesn't want to stay here and let me take care of her. But I know that when I've been ill in the past, I've preferred to be in my own space and my own bed. "Let me just grab my keys, and I'll take you."

"You don't have to do that. I can just get a cab."

"Riley." I place my palm on her cheek, and I swear she pulls back slightly. "I'm not going to send you off in a cab when you're not feeling well."

She gives a slight nod and then stands up. "Okay. Thank you."

The drive to her apartment is silent. I steal glances at her along the way, trying to get a read on her, trying to tell whether or not it is just sickness that has her acting weirdly.

"Do you want me to stay for a little while?" I ask when we pull up to her apartment.

"No, it's okay. I'm just going to be sleeping."

The same disappointment from earlier hits me again. She doesn't want me around her. I get out of the car and help her out of her side, not giving her a choice as to whether or not I walk her up. When we get to her door, she turns toward me, still looking pale.

"Thanks, JD...Jasper."

"Are you sure everything is okay?" I tuck a strand of her hair behind her ear.

She nods. "I'll be fine."

I palm her cheek and lean in for a quick kiss. "I'll call you a little later to see how you're feeling."

"Okay. Thanks." She unlocks her door and whispers, "Bye," before stepping through.

I head back home alone, feeling a lot less happy and a lot less confident about our relationship than I was this morning.

CHAPTER EIGHTEEN

Riley

"Are you sure?" Mia asks from her seat on the couch.

I continue my pacing back and forth, rubbing a sweaty palm on my forehead. As soon as I got home, I called Mia and asked if she could pick me up right away and if I could stay at her place for a few days.

"I don't know, Mia. I mean, I'm pretty sure." I stop for a second, trying to run through everything that has ever been said between us. "He has reminded me of him from the very beginning. His personality. Some of the things he's said about growing up. His voice is similar, if I remember correctly. His hair and eye color are even the same. And seriously, what are the chances that I've met two Jaspers in the past six months?"

"I don't know. Jasper isn't super uncommon. And really,

wouldn't he have told you right when you first met?"

"Right?" I let out a laugh that sounds a little crazy even to my ears. "You'd think."

I have no idea what kind of game he's playing if it *is* really him. He seemed so perfect.

I need to know if it's him.

My phone starts ringing, telling me that JD is calling me. I close my eyes, not that it makes a difference, and let it continue to ring until it goes to voice mail. Tears fill my eyes when I think about how perfect last night was, and then this morning.

"I need to know," I say to Mia. "You've seen Jasper. Would you know if it was him if you saw him again?"

"Yeah. I remember him. But what are you going to do? Ask him to come over while I'm with you?"

I shake my head. "No. I can't see him right now. Well, not *see* him, but you know what I mean. I can't be around him at the moment."

"Okay. What do you have in mind?"

I start pacing again, staying on the same path, so I don't run into anything. "Can you go to where he works?"

"The ultrasound place?"

I exhale a breath. "Yeah."

"You know I would," she says softly. "But what will be my excuse? I can't just go in and ask for an ultrasound to be done."

"I don't know." I rub at my temples. "I don't know. Maybe you could just go and watch the front entrance or something on Monday, around eight-twenty, when he arrives?"

"I can do that. It actually works out perfectly because I don't have any clients booked until nine on Monday morning."

"Okay." I blow out another breath and then feel for the couch to sit down on. "Thank you, Mia."

She pulls me in for a hug. "You're welcome. But you need to calm down until then, though, alright? It's not good for the baby if you're all worked up."

I nod into her shoulder and rub my belly. It has become a habit of mine over the last several months.

"Is it okay if I lay down for a little while?"

I really am not feeling well. As soon as he had said his name, all the contents of my stomach tumbled around like a dryer. Confusion, anger, and uncertainty swirled around. All of a sudden, I wasn't sure of anything. The happy morning I was floating on was pulled out from underneath me.

It almost felt like my time with JD hadn't been real. Was it all a joke? Was he playing me? Or does Jasper really not remember who I am? Did that night mean absolutely nothing to him?

"Of course. The guest bedroom is all set up for you," she says. "Want me to take you there?"

"No. It's fine, thanks." I know Mia's apartment almost as well as my own, so I know exactly where I'm going; the second door on the left in the hallway. There is a little scratch on the wood above the handle.

Even though my mind is racing with a million different scenarios and a million different explanations as to what is going on, I'm still exhausted, so I fall asleep easily.

When I wake up, I feel like I've been sleeping for hours. My phone is chiming from the nightstand with another phone call from JD. *Jasper.* It must be what woke me. I contemplate answering it. JD has been sweet and kind to me, after all, and I was falling for him. Or maybe already had.

But it's all kind of on hold for now until I can figure out the truth. I'm confused, and I think talking to him right now would only make it worse. I know that sounds weird because talking helps resolve issues, but I need to know if it's him first, and I don't feel comfortable asking him outright. I can just imagine that question.

"Hey, were you the guy I had a one-night-stand with months ago?"

No. I'll have to wait until Monday when Mia sees him.

I wait until his message is recorded after he's been sent to voice mail again, and then listen to both of the messages he has left.

"Hey, Riley. Just checking in. Hopefully, you're sleeping and will feel better when you wake up. Talk to you later." My heart squeezes at the sound of his voice.

"Me again. Just a little worried 'cause I haven't heard from you... Just let me know you're okay."

The sincerity in his voice almost has me caving in and calling him back, but until I know whether or not he's really the Jasper from months ago, the father of my baby, I just can't do it. I tell my phone to write out a reply for me.

Me: Hey, sorry. I have been asleep. I'm okay. Just tired. Will take it easy tonight and tomorrow. Thanks for checking in.

A moment later, I get a text in return and have my phone read it to me.

JD: Glad you got some sleep. Would you like me to bring you some dinner?

Me: Thanks, but I'm good. I'm hanging out with my friend, and she will cook us dinner.

JD: Okay.

Now I feel even worse, but I don't know why. I didn't lie at all, but it still feels like I'm lying to him, and he accepted it with a simple 'okay'. Ugh. My brain. My hormones.

Everything just seems out of whack. I just need this weekend to be over with so that Mia can see Jasper and then tell me it's a different guy and that I'm just acting crazy.

Then everything will be good again.

* * *

I told Jordan that I needed a few days off, so I'm just lying on Mia's guest bed on a Monday morning, staring at a ceiling that I can't see, after being woken up by Mia calling.

"It's him."

My mind is still waking up, so it takes me longer than normal to process what she said through the phone. "I'm sorry, what?"

"I said it's him. It's the same Jasper from Fairfield. I just saw him walk into the building. There's no mistaking it."

Even though I somehow knew it was him, I was kind of in denial. I didn't want it to be him because if it wasn't him, then it would mean he was never lying to me or that he didn't simply forget who I was after that night together. It would mean that I didn't have to try to figure out what the hell is going on because how the hell could he not know that it was me?

"I'm sorry, Riley," Mia says. I had totally forgotten that she was still on the phone.

"It's okay," I say slowly, even though it's not. "I'll be okay." I think I'm telling myself that more so than her.

"What are you going to do?"

That is one thing I know for sure. "I have no idea." We hang up after another minute, and I continue to lay in bed.

Jasper texted a couple of times Saturday night and then yesterday. I guess he realized after I didn't answer another one of his calls that I wasn't going to, so he stuck to texting after that.

Besides a "good morning" text earlier, he hasn't written anything else. I keep wondering if he's playing some sort of game. Does he realize I know who he is now? No, none of that makes any sense. He was the one who told me his name was Jasper. He didn't exactly try to hide it. Others called him JD. I was the one who never bothered to find out if it stood for something else.

So, if there are no sinister ulterior motives, then the only other explanation is that he has no idea who I am. He doesn't remember that wonderful night we shared together. He really has no idea that this baby is his.

My stomach churns, and I have to run to the bathroom before I throw up all over Mia and Kyone's floor. I don't generally get morning sickness anymore, but there has been the odd time here and there that I'll get sick. I guess this is one of those times. It probably doesn't help that I haven't eaten breakfast yet, and now it's already lunchtime. After Mia's phone call this morning, I stayed lying on the bed for a few hours with my mind on a continuous loop.

I walk into the kitchen, only to burst into tears when I realize I don't know what food Mia has or where her things are, and I can't cook anything. They were home all weekend and had cooked me food, so I didn't have to worry about it before now.

I collapse into a pitiful bundle on the ground, crying and feeling sorry for myself. I can't even do this one simple thing of feeding myself. How am I going to take care of a baby? I couldn't tell that the guy I've been "seeing" was the same guy I was with in Fairfield. How will I know if I'm even holding my own baby?

My chest starts heaving as I sob uncontrollably about everything. *I can't do anything.* I can't live a life by myself. And I'm not worth remembering. What I consider a connection to someone means nothing to the person I thought I had the connection with. Even my own father, who I loved and adored, completely forgot about me the second he left.

I'm not sure how long I lie here curled up on the floor with my mind pinging back and forth between feeling helpless and thoughts of JD, but I hear the front door open and close and then hear footsteps approaching.

"Oh my goodness, Riley! Are you okay? Should I call an ambulance? What's wrong?"

I hear Mia crouch down next to me. "I can't do anything," I mumble to her.

"You mean, like, you can't move? Does it hurt?"

I shake my head. "No, like I can't even make myself food."

"Oh, geez." She lets out a heavy breath. "I thought something really bad had happened, Riley."

"I'm sorry," I say, sitting up and wiping a tear. "I came out to get something to eat and realized that I couldn't."

"Aw." Mia puts her hand on my arm. "I'm sure that's not all you're upset about."

"No. But I'll be okay." I take in a deep breath and try to push all the negative thoughts away again.

She stands up and pulls me up with her, then hugs me. "I'm sorry about the food thing. I actually had some strawberries and yogurt for you in the fridge. It had some paper on it so you could recognize which container it was, but I completely forgot to tell you when I called earlier."

"That's okay. It's not your fault. I was just having a pity party. What are you doing at home anyway?"

I hear the fridge open and close, then a drawer opening. "I decided to come home for lunch. See how you are doing. I'm glad I did."

"Sorry I scared you before."

"Just don't do that again." She guides me to a seat and makes me sit down. "Here are the strawberries and the yogurt. I'm going to make a couple of sandwiches. If you don't feel like eating one yet, I'll put it in the fridge for you for later."

"Thanks, Mia." I sigh. "You really are the best."

"Don't forget it." She clicks her tongue at me, which is her version of winking at me.

Since I don't really want to think and talk about this whole JD-Jasper situation, I decide to voice to Mia the other thing that has been on my mind today.

"How am I going to do it, Mia? How am I going to raise a baby when I can't even see it? How can I protect it? How can I make it food?"

"Aw, hon." She puts down whatever she has in her hands and walks over to me, taking hold of my hands. "I'm not going to lie and say it won't be hard because it will. But you have us as support and help, and your sister and her family. You'll figure it out, and we will all be there for you. Okay?" I nod my head, but I'm not really overly convinced.

After lunch, Mia heads back to work and leaves me with some easy-access food and instructions to stay off the ground and try not to stress. She said we're going to talk the JD thing out tonight. I wish I wasn't feeling so confused and emotional about it. It feels like it's stopping me from seeing things clearly, stopping me from thinking clearly. Like my brain is foggy.

I jump when I hear my phone start ringing, but it's only Jordan. "Hey," I answer.

"Hey," she says slowly. "So, you gonna tell me what's up yet?"

"I told you I just needed a few days off."

"Yes, you did. But you never said *why*. And I would have thought maybe you wanted to spend a few days off with JD, but then he stopped by briefly today to check if you were okay because he hadn't heard from you."

I close my eyes and lean back on Mia's couch. Guilt slowly presses harder onto my chest. "And what did you tell him?"

"I told him that you weren't in this week and that I hadn't talked to you since Friday but that if something *was* wrong, *I'd* know."

I know the meaning behind her words, and she's expecting an explanation from me. But I don't want to tell her about this mess just yet. I don't want her opinions or 'I told you so's'. I just can't handle it at the moment. I will talk to her about it. Just not yet.

I think of something that is true but not necessarily the reason for all of this. "We were moving pretty fast, and I don't have only myself to think about. I need a few days to think."

"That's a really smart thing to do, Riley," she says softly. "But maybe let JD know that."

"I will." I think. Maybe. Yes, I'll text him that. "How has it been at the restaurant otherwise?" I ask, trying to change the subject.

"It's been busy but not unmanageable, so that's good."

"I'm sorry I bailed on you this week."

"Don't be sorry. As I said, it hasn't been too bad." Her voice turns softer again. "Just do what you need to do, alright? Make sure you take care of yourself. Oh, and come have dinner this week."

"I will. Love you, Jord."

"Love you, too."

I try to keep my mind busy for the rest of the day after

talking to Jordan. I locate a broom and sweep as best as I can. I listen to music. I try to learn some more braille, and I fit a shower and nap in there too. The nap was especially needed since I've slept so restlessly the last couple of nights. I'm sure that hasn't helped with my mixed-up thoughts.

Before I know it, it's already dinner time. Kyone, Mia, and I are sitting around the table eating. I listen to the two of them bantering back and forth and telling each other about their days. I'm so glad they found each other. They're so perfect together. Of course, it makes me think of Jasper, and it makes me sad. I thought we were pretty perfect together as well.

"I hope you don't mind, Riley, but Mia told me a little of what's going down." I shake my head that I don't mind. I know they tell each other everything. "So, this dude is the father but doesn't know it?"

I put my fork down and reach for my water, just holding it in my hands for something to do. "I don't know. I hope that's all it is."

"What do you mean?"

"Well, if he hasn't simply forgotten me, which is a horrible thought as it is, then he's messing with me or something. I don't know why or with what results. But whether he remembers me or not, either way, it's hurtful."

Kyone is quiet again, and I resume eating. I know I need to talk to Jasper. Obviously. I just need to get my emotions under control, and figure out how to approach this, figure out what I need to say.

"You guys were using your middle names on that trip, right?" Kyone asks after a couple of minutes. "Did you give him your middle name?"

"*Yes*. She did!" Mia half shouts. "You totally did, Riley. So maybe he didn't forget. He just thinks you're someone else."

My heart beats faster at the possibility. But how likely is that? "I don't know. If you ran into Kyone somewhere, and he gave you a different name, would you believe he was someone else?"

"No. But it had been, what? Five months since you and Jasper saw each other last? And you were together *one* night."

"Not only that," Kyone chimes in. "But you weren't blind then or pregnant."

"That's right! To him, you're a totally different person."

The realization that they're probably right slams into me. He asked if I had a twin. He said I reminded him of someone.

"Oh my goodness," I bury my face in my hands and speak into my palms. "I'm an idiot. Of course, he thinks I'm someone different." Annoyance at my hormonal brain makes me groan and throw my hands down again. "You know, I've read pregnant women get pregnancy brain. I just didn't realize it would make me more blind to things than I already am."

"Aw, sweetie," Mia puts a hand on my arm. "All of it is a lot to take in. You never thought you'd see Jasper again, and then you do, and you both think each other are different people, and then start dating. I mean, really, that's a great love story right there. Like fate."

I smile for what feels like the first time in days. I guess it is a pretty good story to tell. I still need to talk to Jasper, but maybe everything will work out for us after all.

* * *

It still takes me a few more days to work up the nerve to go and see Jasper at work. Besides the fact that I'm going to be telling him who I am, I'll also be telling him that this baby is his. I'm filled with all sorts of feelings. Excitement at being with him again and knowing that he *is* my Jasper. Anticipation for how he's going to react. And also nervous because he hasn't responded to my text from last night or this morning, telling him I was coming in to see him at lunch.

After talking with Jordan on Monday, I did text Jasper and told him I just needed a few days. But I had assumed that when I contacted him again, he'd reply.

I wipe my sweaty palms on my pants and thank the cab driver as I get out. After a deep breath, I pull open the door to the clinic where Jasper works. I know the front desk is to my left, so I turn in that direction and use my cane to feel the ground in front of me.

"Can I help you?" the receptionist asks.

Great. I recognize that voice as the woman who approached our table that day. What was her name again? Maya?

"Hi. I was hoping to speak to Jasper, er, JD."

"You're Riley, right?"

"Uh, yes," I say, a little confused that she knows my name. Maybe JD told her about me. "I know he usually has lunch around now."

"Listen, do yourself a favor, and don't come back in here again."

The confusion about this woman knowing my name turns to annoyance at her trying to tell me what to do.

"Um, excuse me?"

"You shouldn't be here."

"I just want to see him on his lunch break, okay?"

She sighs loudly, and this time when she speaks, her voice is a lot lower and sounds like she's leaning in closer to me. "I'm trying to be nice here. You're not the first woman to come in here looking for him, alright? And I'm sorry, but you certainly won't be the last."

An uneasy feeling starts to gnaw at my insides. "What do you mean?"

"I mean, you had your turn with him, and now he's onto the next one. Trust me. *I know* how that goes."

No, no, no. It can't be true. "I don't be–"

"Sweetie, he's out to lunch with another woman right now... Hey Dani?" she calls loudly. "Is JD still out with Patricia?"

"Yeah," a voice calls from further away. "Isn't she–"

"Thanks," she says, cutting the person off. "See. I wanted you to see what type of man he is so that you wouldn't cry over him. He's not worth it. I'm really sorry you fell for his act."

My eyes threaten to fill with tears at what she's implying, and I don't want her to see me cry. I stumble backward, almost causing myself and the person behind me to fall to the ground.

"I'm so sorry," I mumble, straightening up as embarrassment skates up my spine.

How many people are standing around us, listening to what she's saying?

"That's okay. Are you alright?" the man asks.

"Yes," I breathe out and then rush to leave.

I need to get a hold of him. I need to talk to him. She has to be lying.

Outside, I lean against the wall and pull out my phone to call him. It's sent to voice mail both times, and then a moment later, I get a text reply from him and have my phone read it to me.

Jasper: Stop calling me.

All the blood in my body runs cold. The food in my stomach threatens to come up. My heart pounds heavily in my chest.

She was right. It was all a lie. The nice guy act was a lie, and I fell for it twice. That's why he never texted me back last night, because he had already moved on and was going out with another woman today.

He's probably been with so many women, and that's why he didn't remember me from months ago. He pursued me *again,* having no idea who I was. And I was easy prey, too. Pregnant, alone, and blind. No wonder he wasn't concerned with any of it. He was never planning on sticking around. He was always planning on getting out as soon as we slept together, and I made it perfectly easy for him by telling him I needed a few days.

I wonder how many women he's done this to?

He acts all sweet and kind just so he can fuck you and then fuck off.

I need to get out of here. I need to forget JD or Jasper ever existed.

CHAPTER NINETEEN

Riley

Mia and I step out of her vehicle. It's raining out, so she rushes over to my side with an umbrella. I can't find it in myself to care if I get wet, though.

The rain reminds me of the movie in the park date I had with Jasper, but I shove it out of my mind the second the memory appears. Mia took the afternoon off from the salon to take me back to my apartment and help get me settled in again.

"Are you sure about this?" Mia links her arm with mine and takes my bag from my other hand.

"Yes. I was only meant to be at your place for a few days. Now it's been just over two weeks. You and Kyone need your space back."

"You know we don't mind having you there one bit. You're

like family."

We start walking toward my building. "Thanks. But I still need to get back to my apartment. Get back to my life. I've had time to wallow. I'm good now."

I've been hiding out at their place for a little over two weeks now, and I ended up taking all that time off of work too. I needed it. Feeling emotionally drained led to feeling physically drained, and I needed to make sure I rested and ate properly for the baby.

Tomorrow, I'll be going back to work. I'll be moving forward again. I'll be continuing on with my life just like I was before I met Jasper again at the ultrasound clinic. I will eventually tell him about the baby because regardless of anything, I still believe he should know. I'll do it before the baby is born, but not right now.

Mia helps me get rid of anything in my fridge that is spoiled and then goes out to grab me a few necessities. I appreciate all the help she's given over the past two weeks. And Jordan as well. I swallowed down my stupid pride and told her everything that was going on. Of course, she went mama bear on me and wanted to go storming into Jasper's workplace, but I repeated the words Maya had said to me when I went there. "He's not worth it."

She went into controlling mode as well. Trying to tell me to move in with her. Telling me that she didn't want me to go anywhere by myself again in case more people like Jasper were around. But after an argument and me storming out of their house, she apologized and told me that she realized that it could have easily happened even if I weren't blind.

I know she was talking about the being used and tossed aside by a player part, but I couldn't help but think that it wouldn't have happened if I could see. I would have recognized him. I wouldn't have felt so needy toward him. And I would have maybe picked up on some facial clues that

I probably missed.

Ever since our fight, Jordan has been supportive, and we've hung out a few times.

By the time Mia gets back, the rain has stopped. I've changed my bedding and have a load of washing on. I've also managed to wipe down anywhere that may have collected dust while I was gone.

"I'll make you something for dinner that you can heat up later. And I'll make sure there are enough leftovers for you to freeze or eat tomorrow if you want."

"Thanks, Mia. What would I do without you?"

"I am pretty amazing." She clucks her tongue. "But so are you, and you would still be a strong independent woman without me around."

"I don't feel so strong and independent lately," I mumble.

"Riley, you're pregnant. That alone gives you, like, *twice* the hormones and emotions or something. You could have easily been a whiny baby, and it would have been normal. But you've plowed through with your head held high."

I think back to that day she found me on the kitchen floor after having a meltdown. Since then, I haven't done anything like that again. In fact, apart from the day that I went to see Jasper at the clinic, I haven't cried at all.

"Speaking of plowing, Kyone and I have been talking about maybe getting pregnant this year."

"*What*? That's so exciting, Mia!" I genuinely smile at her news. She's probably been holding off telling me. "I'm so happy for you."

"Depending on when it happens, our babies will only be two years apart maximum. They can still be best friends."

I laugh. "Or one of us will have a girl, and the other will have a boy. Then they might end up dating."

"Can you imagine?" Mia giggles and starts cooking some chicken. "Are you hoping for either one? Girl or a boy?"

"Mm, I don't actually have a preference. I'll be happy with either." Either one will get all my love, and I'll do all that I can to look after them.

"You're going to be an amazing mom. I can't wait to meet him or her."

Mia stays for a couple more hours and then leaves to do a few errands before heading home. It's nice to be in my own space again. A little quiet, but still nice. I decide to take a bath and play some music. Leaning back in the warm water, I go through a mental list of what I'd like to get this week for the baby's room. I know Jordan would love to come with me, so I'll ask her tomorrow at work.

After another hour or so, I start craving some ice cream. Unfortunately, it wasn't in the necessities that Mia brought for me. I try to ignore it, but the craving only gets stronger.

"Fine, you win," I say to my belly, giving it a rub. "I guess I'm walking to the store."

Instead of getting a tub, I get one that I can eat right now and sit on the bench outside the store to enjoy it. The air smells fresh, and the sun hasn't started its descent yet, so I don't mind sitting for a little while.

Just as I'm taking my last bite, I feel someone sit down with a thump on the other end of the bench.

"So, it is true. The almighty Riley is pregnant and blind. I didn't believe it at first, but, well, here you are."

I grit my teeth. Of all the people to run into, it had to be him. "What do you want, Pax?"

"What do I want? Funny that you should ask me that now. You didn't care what I wanted when I wanted you to give me another chance."

"You cheated on me," I growl. "Why would I want to give

you another chance?"

"I made a mistake!"

I laugh. "How many mistakes, Pax? How many times did you accidentally cheat on me, and with how many women?"

He huffs out a breath. "It wasn't like that."

I roll my eyes, getting fed up with this conversation. "It doesn't matter. It was over a year ago now. I've moved on. I'm sure you've moved on too, plenty of times."

"Moved on." He chuckles, but there is no humor in it. "I heard you don't even know who the father is."

I know he's just trying to get to me. I *do* know who the father is, and there's no way he would know anything about Jasper and our story. I'm not too sure where he heard about me being pregnant or that I'm blind. We didn't have a lot of the same friends, but I guess it's not exactly a secret around here.

"How'd you get blind anyway?" I try to ignore him, but he just keeps going. "Pretty sucky. How are you going to look after a kid when you can't even see it? You'll never know if it's bleeding. If it's all red from overheating or if it's blue because it can't breathe. You won't even know what you're putting in its mouth."

I keep my face stoic and continue facing forward. I don't want to satisfy him with a reaction, but on the inside, I'm dying. He's hitting every one of my insecurities, bringing up all of the things I've already thought and stressed about.

"I'm not trying to be an asshole."

Bullshit! "Yes, you are."

"I'm not. I'm just curious."

"Well, you don't need to be. My life has nothing to do with you, so just piss off."

He chuckles again. I have no idea what I ever saw in him.

I guess his asshole wasn't showing as much back then. Not until I broke up with him and didn't take him back when he wanted me to. That's when the nastiness showed up.

I feel him get up. "Still stubborn, I see. Well, good luck, Riley. You're going to need it."

It doesn't feel as nice sitting out here anymore. I get up and walk home as fast as possible, using my cane to help me not trip over. By the time I make it inside, my chest is heaving, and tears are threatening at the back of my eyes.

"Arggh!"

Why did I let him get to me? I should have walked away as soon as I heard him speak. I knew nothing good would come out of his mouth. When he doesn't get what he wants, he cuts you down.

I reach for my bag and dig into one of the pockets, looking for the card I was given a little while back. It has a QR code on it that dials a phone number instead of sending me to a website or something. I flip it over in my hands a few times. I didn't think I'd ever use it, but now, I think it might be a good idea.

CHAPTER TWENTY

Jasper

Four weeks.

Four long, miserable, lonely weeks.

Four weeks since I had lunch with my mother, who randomly appeared in the city one day because my father apparently had an appointment with a specialist here.

Four weeks since I walked back into work from that awkward lunch, and Maya told me Riley had been in to see me. But it wasn't a good message she had left for me. Maya told me she said that she had time to think and that we were done, and she didn't want to see or hear from me anymore. A clean break. That's what she'd apparently asked for.

My phone had disappeared the day before while I was at work, so I didn't even have her number to call or text right away. I had immediately left work again to buy a new cell, and then I stole her number from her file. I wrote out at least ten different texts but then deleted them all. I brought up her name a number of times to call but never pressed it. I didn't want to have an awkward conversation over the phone or through texts, especially since Maya was adamant about her not wanting to be contacted.

To say I was devastated is putting it mildly. I didn't want to let it go, so I went to her apartment to talk to her in person. She never answered the door, no matter what I said through it. I tortured myself by going there, again and again, that first week. But after the seventh time going there and getting no response, her neighbor told me to get lost and said that she would have contacted me if she wanted to see me. I stopped going there after that, especially since he seemed like he'd call the cops if I didn't.

That night, I caved and called her phone, but it was disconnected.

A life with a family filled with love, happiness, and adventures, was so close I could taste it. I could feel it with the tips of my fingers. But it wasn't just the *life* that I wanted. It was *her*. She made me feel all of the things that I didn't feel while growing up.

Wanted, needed, excited, and loved.

And then it was all taken away.

Shay opened the lid on all of those feelings that night.

Then Riley tipped out the box before walking away.

"Are you gonna play a card or just stare at them all night?"

My eyes come back into focus, and I actually see the cards in my hands again. "Fold."

"Took you long enough to decide that," Patrick's friend, Mavis, says.

"Give him a break. He's going through some stuff," Patrick tells him.

"Oh Yeah?" Patrick's other friend, Dante, pipes up. "By the looks of him, women stuff."

I don't answer. I just pick up my glass of whiskey and swallow a large portion down, ignoring the burn that slides down my throat.

"You should come with us to ladies' night tomorrow night," Mavis says as he shoves a handful of peanuts in his mouth.

"No, thanks."

"C'mon." He elbows me. "You could meet someone else. Turn that frown upside down."

"I said fuckin' *no*."

Everyone is silent for a moment before Patrick speaks up. "No offense, JD, but you used to be a nice, quiet guy. Now you're a quiet asshole."

I scrub a hand over my face. "Sorry."

"Nah, man. It's all good. Now you're just more like the rest of us." He chuckles, and then the other guys join in.

I'm not sure that I want to be just like the rest of them. I'm not sure I want to go through this again, either. Maybe I'm doomed to be alone until I die, just like my brother.

"I do feel sorry for you, man," Patrick says in a more serious tone. "But maybe it's for the best. Her being pregnant brought extra complications and obligations you don't need."

Mavis' eyebrows go up. "Whoa, she was pregnant?"

I nod. "It never mattered to me."

Patrick wins the hand and drags his winnings from the middle of the table. "You do actually seem like the family type."

I shrug. I thought I could be.

"What about the baby-daddy?"

I shrug again. I never asked about him. I figured she'd tell me when she was ready. Who knows, maybe she's decided to get back together with him?

"I dated a girl with a kid once." This comes from Dante. He leans his elbows on the table, looking thoughtful. "The dad was never in the picture, so he didn't matter."

"What happened?" Patrick asks as he deals out the cards again.

"Honestly, I don't remember. She was a nice girl. I think it just fizzled out."

"She probably got tired of seeing your ugly mug," Mavis says, throwing a peanut at Dante's face.

His words, of course, make me think of how Riley has never seen me. And for some reason, the thought of her never recognizing me from the next guy if she ever got her sight back makes me sad again.

I stay for another hour, mostly just listening to them chatting back and forth. Then, instead of going straight home, I find myself pulling up outside The Reading Nook. I don't get out, though. I stay sitting in my car, staring at the front door. I don't know why. I know she's not going to come out of it. I've tried coming here to read a few times, but I always end up just looking at the same page and reading the same paragraph over and over, not absorbing a thing.

After a few minutes, I reverse out of the parking spot and drive home alone, again. The first thing I see when I walk through the door to my townhouse is the gift bag sitting on the table in my entryway. It has the little plush football I had got for Riley's baby, as well as the little outfit that says "MAMA'S BOY" on it.

I pull out the tiny football and roll it between my hands. It's barely bigger than my palm. Is it weird for me to feel sad that I'll never meet him? Probably. But I do feel sad. Shaking my head, I stuff it back in the gift bag and put the bag on the top shelf of my closet.

* * *

Another miserable week passes. I feel like I'm just going through the motions of everything. Wake up, eat breakfast in my quiet home, get ready for work, repeat the same words and instructions to all of my patients, try to muster up a smile and fake at least a tiny bit of happiness for them. Meanwhile, I'm jealous of the families that they have or will have.

Then at the end of every day, I go to my quiet home once again, eat dinner, and go to sleep. Only to get up and do the same thing all over again.

Maya sits down at the table I'm eating lunch at. "Hey, JD. How are you doing?"

"Good."

"No, you're not, but that's okay. You'll get there. And I'll be waiting for when you want to talk."

Her hand lands on my arm. She's been very kind and understanding over the past several weeks and hasn't given up on talking to me even when I haven't said much in return.

Maybe she's someone I should be giving a chance to. Maybe I should be seeing where it could go with her. Being stuck on Shay first and then Riley even more so, hasn't done me any good. And Maya looks nothing like either of them, so maybe that will be good. The more I think about it, the more I convince myself that I *should* try.

But when I look at her face, I feel absolutely nothing. There is no spark, no desire to get to know her better. And the feel of her hand on my arm does nothing for me. In fact, it feels *wrong*.

Pulling my arm away from her, I stand up. "Excuse me. I need to get back to work."

"JD." She sighs but doesn't say anything more when I don't answer.

At the end of the day, I walk out without talking to anyone once again, but just before I reach my car, I hear my name being called out. I turn to see Patrick jogging toward me.

"JD, wait up."

When he reaches me, he doesn't say anything right away. He just shuffles on his feet and scratches his jaw like he does when he's deciding whether or not to say something.

"What?" I demand impatiently.

He takes a few steps, stops, and turns around. "Alright, shit." He blows out a breath. "Riley is upstairs."

Every one of my muscles tenses at hearing her name while my insides come alive. I'm at war with myself, curious but indifferent, happy but angry. But what was the rest of his sentence?

"What the hell do you mean she's upstairs? In your clinic?"

He gives one head nod. "Yeah. She came in for the procedure... the experimental one I told you about."

"What the fuck, man!" I grab at his shirt. "How could you do that? She's pregnant. It's not safe!"

He pushes me off of him. "It's plenty safe!" Then, with a more calm voice, he continues. "It's done in such a way that I don't need sedatives to do it."

I huff out a breath. "It's still experimental. What if it doesn't work, and she goes completely blind? What if something goes wrong?"

"She knew the risks when she agreed to it."

"How did she even find out about it?" He looks off to the side. "Dammit, Patrick! It was that day in the hallway. You gave her a card, didn't you?" I shove my hand through my hair. "Why didn't you tell me?"

"I didn't have to tell you shit. And I didn't have to tell you this now, either. I *shouldn't* have."

"Then why did you?"

He paces a few steps again. "I don't know. She just...she seemed kind of like you, man. Not happy. And she's alone. She's staying in the extra-care rooms. You know, for seniors or people that live alone that need the extra help."

I chew on the inside of my cheek, contemplating. I can't believe she's there, right above my workplace.

"When does she have the procedure?"

He looks at the ground. "We did it today. She'll be there for a few days now for monitoring since she doesn't have any help at home."

"Do you...do you know if it was successful?" I ask.

"No. We won't until a couple of days when we take the patches off." I nod in acknowledgment. "Are you going to go see her now?" he asks. "I can tell Macy to let you in."

I look up at the building, wondering which window might be her room, and then back at him. "No."

"What? Why not? What are you going to do?" he asks with a confused look.

"Nothing." I turn around and continue on toward my car, leaving him standing in the parking lot.

She wanted to end things between us. She wanted me cut off. She doesn't want to see me.

CHAPTER TWENTY-ONE

Riley

For the second day in a row, when I open my eyes, I can see. Not clearly. Things still look a bit fuzzy, like I'm looking through someone else's prescription glasses, but I can *see* that it's morning. I can *see* the paneled ceiling above me in the room I'm staying in at the clinic.

Yesterday, I could *see* the handsome doctor Patrick, who did the procedure, and the blonde nurse that was with him. Color. I can *see* color. It's not as vibrant as before the accident, but I can still make out the colors, even if they are dull.

When they first took the patches off, I wanted to go running through the streets, yelling to whoever would listen that I could see again. It was such a surreal experience, especially since I had already accepted my fate of never seeing again.

Dr. Patrick Maze told me that I had to stay here for a couple of days, though, so there was no leaving here just yet. Since it is experimental, they're still unsure of possible side effects and wanted to monitor me.

Staying in here a couple of more days was hardly an issue considering what I've gained back; the ability to see where I'm going, see what I'm putting in my mouth, and see my baby when it's born. I can start my schooling to become a nurse. I can drive. So, yeah, a couple more days was nothing.

I turn my head to the left, where there is a window, and I can *see* that it's a sunny day. A bird flies by the window, and I smile at it. I find that I've done that a lot since the patches were removed. Just seeing the simplest things make me happy.

When I first looked in the mirror, I was surprised at how different I appeared. Although I can't see as clearly as I once could, I could still tell that my face looked fuller, my skin looked clearer, and my hair looked wavier. I wonder if I would have still noticed these things now if I had looked in the mirror every day for the past several months.

Seeing my belly for the first time was an amazing experience as well. Knowing I'll actually get to see him or her with my own eyes makes me tear up every time I think about it. It's a gift that I will not be taking for granted. I smile down at my stomach. Not long now.

Something to my right catches my attention, and I turn to see a man sitting in a chair against the wall. A beautiful man who, besides looking a little tired, looks just how I remember.

"Jasper," I whisper.

He doesn't answer at first. He just continues to sit there

with his elbows on his thighs and hands clasped under his chin, looking at me. After a beat, he gives a head nod, and I realize he's giving me confirmation that he *is* Jasper because, to him, I've never seen him before.

"What are you doing here?"

He gets up and walks over to the window, rapping his knuckles on the window sill a few times before turning back to me.

"I wanted to see for myself how you were doing."

I almost scoff at him but manage to hold it back. Having him here in this room and *seeing* him again is throwing me off. I can't tell if I want to rip the band-aid off, tell him this baby is his, and then tell him to get lost. Or ask him why? Why did he make me fall for him and then toss me aside like yesterday's newspaper? Why did he make me believe in us, believe we could be something, and then forget about me? It was cruel.

At the same time, he also made me believe in myself. At the time, he made me believe that I could still do a lot in my life as a blind person. So, as much as I'm angry and upset with him, I also want to thank him for that. I can't say whether or not I would have gone through with this procedure if he hadn't left me. But I don't regret it.

"I also wanted to . . ." He takes a deep breath before continuing. "I wanted closure. I wanted to hear it from you. Find out what went wrong."

"What?" Is he for real? I swing my legs over the side of the bed to stand up because you can't face someone down when you're lying down. "What do you mean 'what went wrong'?"

"Exactly what I said," he says, crossing his arms across his chest.

It distracts me for a second. I remember running my hands over his arms and how smooth his skin was, the bulges in his muscles. And then I also remember the tattoos that are hidden beneath his clothes. Ugh, concentrate.

"How about you not returning my texts when I said I wanted to see you and talk with you? How about me coming in to see you at work and your previous *toy* Maya, informing me that you were out with another woman for lunch and that you were already done with me? How about ignoring my calls and then telling me to stop texting me? Not even bothering to talk to me in person." I place a finger to my lips. "Yeah, I think all of *that* is where it *went wrong*."

He stares at me like I'm crazy and has no idea what I'm talking about. "I'm sorry, she *what*?" His arms drop to his sides, and he looks down at the ground shaking his head. "None of that makes any sense. The only other woman I've had lunch with in the past six weeks, hell, the past six *years*, is my mother. And that was the day that I walked back into work, and Maya told me that you had been in to see me to end it. She said that *you* didn't want to see *me* or hear from me again. I never ended it with you."

What? I close my eyes, trying to absorb all that he's just told me. Could he be lying?

"Are you serious?" I ask.

"Completely."

I nibble on my lip. "What is your mother's name?"

"Patricia," he answers. "Why?"

"Oh my goodness." My eyes pop open again. "That's the name Maya gave me. Only she skipped the part of who she was." I purse my lips. "But . . . but I got a text from you afterward, telling me to stop texting me."

He shakes his head. "That wasn't from me. My phone went missing. I didn't have one for almost two days. I had to go buy a new one. The last text I got from you was when you said you needed a few days. And I replied, 'okay, whatever you need.'"

We stare at each other for a minute, the reality of the situation sinking in. We both thought the other had ended it. We were both *told* the other had ended it. All this time, all this heartbreak. It was caused by Maya.

"Why would she do this? Did you really mess her up that bad when you ended things with her?"

Jasper lets out a sigh and steps in front of me, placing his hands on my shoulders. "Riley, I was never with her, *ever*. I told you that already. She obviously really wants to be with me, though. But I don't. I haven't been with anyone else in months, and before that, it was even longer."

I close my eyes again, trying to keep my tears away, trying to control the emotions flooding through me. They've been a little harder to contain lately, but today they feel almost impossible.

"So, you didn't say any of that stuff? You still wanted to be with me?"

"Look at me," Jasper says softly, and I do. "I was falling for you. I thought... I thought we were really good together. Of course, I still wanted to be with you."

His face is so open and honest, and all of my feelings for him come rushing to the surface. The feelings from our night together months ago mix and swirl with the more intense feelings from our time together more recently.

I can't believe that I get to see his face again, his expressive brown eyes, his black hair. He looks perfect. My mind starts connecting all of the information that I know between JD and Jasper, how he's kind, how he likes to be touched, how he's quiet, but with me, he talks more.

How could I doubt that he was being anything other than genuine? How could I believe the words of a stranger? Well, the text had come from his phone, so it had *appeared* to be him.

A single tear that I'm unable to stop trickles down my cheek, and Jasper wipes it away. "I was falling for you too, Jasper." He smiles so big, the relief on his face so evident. He starts to lean in for a kiss, but I hold up a hand to stop him. I still have more to say. "Wait, there's something I need to tell you first."

I turn away from his furrowed brow and step toward the window, needing a little distance from him while I speak.

"You know that I had an accident that caused my blindness, but I don't think I ever told you *when* it was. I could actually see quite perfectly just seven months ago." I rub my belly before continuing. "I was driving, talking to my sister on speakerphone in my car, when I was t-boned in that intersection. My sister and I had just been talking about an amazing night I had spent with an amazing man in a small town where I had gone for a bachelorette weekend with some friends. I had given that man my middle name because that's what we had been doing all weekend. It was our rules."

I turn to face him to watch his reaction. He doesn't say anything, but he fidgets and grips the back of his neck while looking at the ground. I can see his chest moving faster, his breaths picking up speed as he connects the dots in his head. Emotions flicker across his face. He *knows* where this is going.

"Do you know what my middle name is, Jasper?" I watch his Adam's apple move up and down as he swallows.

He doesn't answer right away, rubbing a hand across his mouth. "Shay," he finally says quietly.

The side of my lip tips up. "Yeah. I didn't know it was you at first. Not until you told me your name was Jasper." He glances up at me, nodding as he takes it in. "I always thought there were similarities, but without seeing your face, and thinking your name was JD, that's all they were, *similarities*.

When you told me your name and my friend Mia confirmed it was definitely you, I was confused and hurt. I didn't know what to think. I thought that maybe you were playing me, or you just *forgot* me. That's why I needed a few days to think."

He shakes his head, his eyes widening. "How could I forget you? Every time I saw you at first, I saw Shay. The very first time I saw you was actually at The Reading Nook. I noticed you by the windows, and I was so shocked and happy to see you again. But when I came closer, you didn't react. At the time, I thought you'd forgotten *me*. Then it was actually your sister who walked up to you and called you Riley, and I saw that you were blind. I assumed it mustn't be you."

It was him that time at The Reading Nook. That time when I saw the person come toward me and I had had that reaction to him. It was him all along.

Jasper takes a couple of steps closer to me. "And then you came in for an ultrasound..." He suddenly trails off and looks down at my stomach, then back at my face, and then at my stomach again. Like he's working something out. "He's...he's mine?" he chokes out.

His eyes get a glossy sheen to them as emotions fill him, and several tears trail down my face as I nod. He quickly closes the distance between us and pulls me in close, burying his head in my hair.

"All this time. This is...I can't believe it." He pulls back and cups my cheeks, pressing a gentle kiss to my lips. Then his eyes roam over my face like he's just seeing me for the first time. "And you can see again," he says like he's just realizing.

I laugh through my tears. "Yes. I can see you."

Shaking his head, he says in awe, "This is nothing like I had thought today would turn out."

"So you're...happy about this?"

"Are you kidding me? Yes, I'm happy. I mean... assuming you want to be with me?"

There is no question about it. "Of course I do. It's funny. It kinda feels like we've known each other forever already."

"It does. And, yes. I'm very happy."

He presses a kiss on my forehead.

"I went from living a lonely life..."

A kiss to my lips.

"To thinking about Shay every day..."

A kiss on my cheek.

"To thinking about Riley every day..."

A kiss on my other cheek.

"But they were both you..."

A kiss on my nose.

"So really, I've been thinking about you every single day since I met you..."

A kiss to my chin. "And now you're here, and you're carrying my baby."

Jasper's hands drop to my belly, and he caresses it so gently, like he's handling expensive china.

"Yes," I whisper.

In the next breath, he presses his lips to mine in a searing kiss. I open up to him immediately, allowing his tongue into my mouth. I curl my arms around his neck and kiss him back with all the passion and love that I feel for him. All this time lost, and yet my feelings are stronger than before.

His hands move to touch me all over. It's always like that, like he can't decide where he wants to feel first. But then he slides his hands around my lower back and pulls me closer so that I can feel his erection.

"I can't stop touching you," he says as his lips glide over

my jaw. "I really want to be inside you right now."

I'm so turned on as well. I can't think of anything more I'd like at this very moment than to be intimate with him. To show him how I feel. But we're not somewhere private.

"We can't do it here at the clinic, on this hospital bed."

He stops his kissing for a second. "You're right. Not on the bed. I could just bend you over and fuck you from behind while you lean against it."

I let out a laugh at his words. "I haven't heard you talk like this before. I think I like it."

Jasper leans his forehead against mine. "'I can't help it. Just knowing that you're the same woman that I was with that night does something to me. The thought of you carrying my baby makes me hard...but *seeing* it?" He looks down at my stomach and shakes his head. "It makes me feel like a caveman."

This time it's me that pulls him down and crashes our lips together. I slide my fingers through his hair like I know he loves and try to get as close as possible. Who cares where we are? After all this time and the misunderstandings, I need this.

I turn around just like he said and bend over the bed, pressing my ass into his groin. Jasper lets out the hottest-sounding groan and digs his fingers into my hips, pressing me harder into him. I can't tell if it's the pregnancy hormones or if it's simply Jasper that has me so close to the edge with only the contact through our clothes.

He releases my hips, sweeps my hair to the side, and places his hands on top of mine on the bed, threading our fingers together. Soft lips press soft kisses on my neck and shoulder. It contradicts his hard dick grinding hard into my ass. I'm so lost in the moment that I almost don't hear the knock at the door.

"Jasper," I whisper.

"Mm," he says, moving to nibble my ear.

"Jasper," I say again. "There was a knock on the door."

He pauses what he's doing, and we both listen to see if the person is still there or if they left. They won't enter without my permission, but they *can*. The door doesn't lock. That realization has me coming out of the haze of lust.

I stand up straighter, only remembering now that I'm still in my pajamas when I look down to start fixing them. Oh well. The person knocks again, and Jasper takes a step away to adjust himself. It's probably Patrick. Hopefully, I'll be able to go home today.

"Come in," I call out. Jasper and I share a small smile right before the door opens.

Patrick comes walking in and does a double-take when he sees Jasper. "JD, I wasn't expecting to see you in here." Jasper gives a head nod, and the side of his lips tip up. "Everything okay?" Patrick asks, looking between us.

"Yes," Jasper answers, moving closer to me again and placing an arm around my shoulders. It amazes me how he can talk so much with me one minute and then go back to a quiet man with short answers the next.

There's a hint of a smile on Patrick's lips as he looks between us. "It's about time. You know he's been asking me for updates on you every day?" Patrick says to me.

"Is that right?" I look up at Jasper, so happy to be able to actually see him. So happy that we've figured out all that went wrong.

Jasper slides his hand down and gives my hip a little squeeze. "Yes."

"He was worried for you. Worried that there might be some kind of bad side effect."

"Even though you thought I left you?" I question.

"Of course," Jasper says quietly. "I still cared about you."

"Well, I'm glad you two have things figured out again. How about I check and see how things look, and then if all is good, you should be able to take her home today."

"Do you mind taking me home?" I ask Jasper. "If you have to work, that's okay. I'll just get a cab or something." Suddenly the thought of him going to work where Maya is, and knowing what she did to us, has me feeling uneasy again.

"No. I took the day off. I wasn't sure how things would go when I saw you. But now that I know everything." He puts a hand on my belly. "I'm not letting you out of my sight today."

Patrick gives him a quizzical look, glancing between me, Jasper, and his hand on my belly. He doesn't ask anything, though. Jasper might tell him about it later. I got the impression that they were friends the first time I met Patrick, and stating that he's glad we have things figured out suggests he knows that there was something to figure out in the first place.

"Okay, thank you."

Jasper kisses me once again. It's like he can't help doing it every few minutes. Like he needs to feel and touch me, needs to know that I'm still here. Not that I mind at all. I just snuggle in closer to him, not caring that Patrick is watching us.

When Patrick clears his throat, Jasper and I pull apart, and I sit up on the edge of the bed, ready for him to check my eyes. I take Jasper's hand in mine. I know that there are still things that we need to discuss, but I also know that I will never let him go again.

CHAPTER TWENTY-TWO

Jasper

I can't help looking over at Riley again. A soft smile plays at the corners of her lips while she looks out the window. I can't imagine the utter joy she must be feeling at being able to see again. She's eagerly taking in everything around us. Watching people talk and laugh on the sidewalk, staring at the colorful flowers in the pots along the street. Anything and everything grabs her attention as we drive to my place.

"You're staring again." She grins while still looking out the window. "You should watch the road."

I guess she didn't miss the fact that I've constantly been looking at her. "I can't help it," I say, focusing back on the road.

Patrick gave her the all-clear to leave, but she'll still have to go in for weekly appointments for the next month at least to monitor if there are any changes. I know he was really curious about our story, but I would rather leave him hanging and spend more alone time with Riley than stay there explaining the whole thing to him. I'm still a little angry with him for doing something that was experimental on Riley, but seeing her so happy with the results now, lessens the anger I had a little.

"You said he," she says suddenly.

"Huh?" I take a quick glance back over to Riley, who is now looking at me.

"You said *'he's* mine'. I thought at first you were just saying it like some guys do when they *want* it to be a boy. But you weren't doing that, were you? You saw it was a boy during the ultrasound, didn't you?"

"Shit," I say quietly, turning to look out the other window. I can feel the tips of my ears heat up. I didn't mean to do that. I wasn't even thinking when I said it. "I'm really sorry, Riley. I didn't mean to tell you."

She's quiet, and I really don't want to look over and see her angry or upset face. I feel terrible already. I know she wanted to wait to find out.

The silence in here starts killing me after another minute, so I risk another glance at her. Thankfully, it's not anger I see when I look at her. She's leaning back against the headrest, looking at me with a smile on her face and tears in her eyes.

"We're having a boy," she says softly.

Her words almost make me lose it. *We're* having a boy. It's not like I intended on making a baby with her that night, but I'm not even a little bit upset about it. I hadn't been thinking about having a child when I met her as *Shay*, but

I definitely started thinking about it after I met her again as *Riley*, and the thought of having a family with her was appealing.

"So, you're not mad?"

"No. I'm not mad at all." She places a hand on my arm. "I'm so incredibly happy right now, Jasper. And I bet he'll look exactly like you."

My heart expands a hundred times in my chest, feeling like it's going to burst. I may not have had the love and affection I craved as a kid, but I definitely feel it for this baby. Even before I knew he was mine, I felt it. I can't wait to shower him with so much love. He will never have to question how I feel about him.

And Riley . . . god, I feel so much love for her as well. I will try to give her everything I possibly can. She has gone through most of this pregnancy alone, and I feel bad about that. But she will no longer be alone. She'll never be alone again if I have my way.

I still find it a little funny how the whole time, I had been thinking the baby's father was a jerk for not being there for Riley, and it was me the whole time.

And I can't help but wonder what would have happened if I hadn't gone in there today. She'd have been released, maybe caught a cab home to her apartment alone, and gone on with her life. We wouldn't have found out about what Maya did to us. And I wouldn't know about the baby right now.

"Were you going to tell me?" I ask after a minute.

"What do you mean?" she asks.

"If I didn't come in there today, would you have told me about the baby?"

"Oh. Yes, I would have. I wouldn't have kept him away from you unless I thought he was in danger." She turns her body, so she's facing me better. "I actually did try to tell you before I met you as JD. In an email."

"An email?" I look over at her when we stop at a red light.

She nods, and a slight blush hits her cheeks. "Yeah, I took a piece of paper with an email address on it from your wallet when I left your hotel room. I knew there was only a slight chance that it was yours, but I wrote to that address anyway and never received anything back."

I lean my head back and let out a groan at how mixed up our situation got. "That *was* my email address."

"What?"

The light turns green, and I continue driving. "I made it two or three days before I flew out to Fairfield because my other one got hacked, and I needed one for a flower order I placed online for my mother. I figured I'd use it for people I met in Fairfield or family friends that might want to stay in contact instead of giving them my phone number. I wrote it down on a little piece of paper in case I forgot what it was 'cause the numbers after JTD were random. Nobody asked to keep in contact, though. They were too upset about my brother, which was understandable. When I couldn't find the paper, I didn't bother trying to remember it and log in because it didn't matter."

"Well, damn," she says, shaking her head. "Guess maybe I should have taken a picture of it instead."

"If I'd gotten anything from you, I would have come for you. Not just because of the baby." I reach over and take her hand in mine. "But for you. I think, no matter how many times we met as strangers, I'd still fall in love with you each time."

We pull up to my home a second later, and as soon as I turn the engine off, Riley pulls my head over to her side and speaks over my lips. "For someone who doesn't usually say a whole lot, you certainly say a lot of the right things."

I close the tiny space between our mouths and kiss her deeply. Nibbling, sucking, and tasting her lips. As soon as she lets out a little moan, I pull back. "Come on, let's go inside."

Nodding, she turns and opens the passenger door, grabbing her bag before she gets out and closes it again. I have to remind myself that she can see now and doesn't need me to guide her inside. It might take a little getting used to. On our way to the car earlier, I had told her that there was a step ahead of us. All she did was smile up at me and continue walking.

"So this is where you live, huh?"

"This is home." Maybe your home one day too, I silently add.

"I still can't believe we were both from here, and we were in Fairfield on the same weekend."

"I know."

Riley's eyes start roving around as soon as we walk through the door to my home. I wonder if it's anything like she had pictured in her head. She spins around once and then lands her eyes on me as I walk up to her.

Her smile is bright when she looks up at me, and I wrap my hands loosely around her back, pulling her close. "What are you thinking?" she asks, tilting her head to the side.

"I'm thinking... how happy I am. How amazing you are. How good you look here, in my home." A cute blush hits her cheeks, and I continue. "I'm thinking about how much I missed you. How much I wanted the baby to be mine, and he is." I give her a quick kiss. "I'm also thinking about how I want to peel off your clothes and kiss you all over."

"Mm." Riley closes her eyes and grips my shirt in her fists. "Jasper," she whispers. "Can I feel you?" Her eyes pop open again. "*All* of you?" She's repeating the words she said to me the night she was here.

"Yes."

Glancing at the couch behind me, she gives a little push for me to sit down, then she lowers herself onto her knees between my legs. I'm already hard and need to adjust myself. Her eyes sparkle with delight as she watches me do it.

It's going to be hard for me not to reach for her immediately. I clench my hands into fists and keep them pasted to my thighs.

Riley places her hands on my forearms first and then slides them slowly up my arms like she did that night. This time she watches her hands move over my skin every step of the way. Moving back down to my clenched fists, she peels each finger open and then traces along my palms with her much smaller fingers. She's killing me with her touches, driving me more and more crazy with need.

Instead of continuing up my arms again, she reaches for the hem of my shirt, and I lean forward to help her take it off. Her eyes land on my ink, and she immediately brings her hands up to trace over the patterns.

"I missed seeing these."

Every stroke of her fingers over my skin drives me wild. It heats up my body a thousand degrees. After a few more seconds, I snap. Grabbing her behind the neck, I bring our mouths together, trapping her hands between us. I kiss her without restraint, showing her how badly I want her, how badly I need her. I kiss her like she's the air I need to breathe, and she kisses me back just as fiercely, letting out little moans of pleasure.

When I finally pull back, her lips are pink and puffy, and her eyes are filled with lust. I reach for her top and whip it up over her head, then take a moment to feel over her smooth belly. *My baby.* As I press kisses all over her soft skin, I reach around to undo her bra. My mouth waters at the sight of her breasts in front of me. They've grown since the last time I saw them.

"Beautiful." I lean forward and take one into my mouth, swirling my tongue around while playing with the other. "Mmm," I groan.

"Jasper," she gasps, threading one of her hands through my hair.

The feel of it sends a shiver through my body. I'm hungry for more. She's still kneeling between my legs, so I help her stand up, and then slowly, I slide her pants down to the ground. Staring at her beautiful naked body standing in front of me feels like the most precious gift has been presented to me.

She watches me with a heated gaze as I slide to my knees before her, nudge her legs apart, and then lean forward to have a taste of her. I can't see her face because of her baby belly, but if the sounds she's making and her hands in my hair are any indication, she's enjoying it.

I've only ever done this once in college, and it was more just to try it out. An experimental transaction with a woman who hung around the same tattoo artists I did. There were no feelings involved. And while I enjoyed it, it was nothing special.

This, though, I am *loving*; her taste, her sounds. I grab her ass and pull her closer, devouring her like a starving man. She's bringing out this primal side of me, and I'm feeling a little crazed. I use my tongue, flicking it back and forth over her clit. And then add my fingers to help bring her to climax. Her whole body shakes as she comes, and she has to use my shoulders to hold herself up.

Finally, after I feel like I've had my fill, I push myself back onto the couch and bring her down to sit on my lap, laying kisses on her skin while she comes down from her high. Riley doesn't stay sitting still for very long, though. Her hands move to the button of my pants, and then she scoots back so she can pull them down. I lift my hips and shove them down for her, pulling her back to me a second later.

"The bigger I get, the harder this will be," she says, moving to straddle me.

I lean into her again, running my nose along her shoulder and up her neck. "As long as you're comfortable."

"Mm, very."

I claim her mouth again, feeling consumed by her. I'll never have enough of her. Excitement pumps through my veins at the fact that she's here with me again.

I lift Riley up by her hips and position myself underneath, desperate to connect our bodies. She sinks down onto me at a painfully slow rate. Once she's fully seated, I glance up to see her watching me with parted lips. I lift her up again, sliding almost all the way out, and then thrust back in at the same time I pull her down. It causes her mouth to open further and a gasp to escape her. I repeat it over and over, watching as pleasure takes over her features.

I move my hands to feel her wherever I can touch, her breasts, her neck, her back, but my eyes stay fixed on her face. My hips never stop pumping into her. When I know she's close again, I pull her face to mine for another kiss. Her hair is like a curtain around us. Keeping us enclosed in this bubble of ecstasy.

Releasing her lips, I kiss up the side of her neck, nibbling on her earlobe. I feel her tensing up, ready to explode, so I pull back to watch it. Her eyes never leave mine, and even if I wanted to, I couldn't look away while she comes undone. It's a beautiful sight that will be forever etched into my brain.

"Jasper." My name is barely a whisper on her lips, but I hear it loud and clear. Everyone else can call me JD, but Jasper is for her.

Pleasure fires through me. Tingles spread up my spine as her fingers tug through my hair first and then run down to my chest, brushing over my nipples. I've held on as long as possible, but I'm so close to losing control now.

My thrusts become erratic, and I pound up into her even harder. I try to say something to her, but I can't. I try to hold back, but I can't. I want to close my eyes, but I can't.

As if she knows what will instantly push me over the edge, Riley reaches for my hands and brings them to her stomach while she grinds down on me. "This is yours," she whispers.

I lose it. The sounds of my release fill the room as I come deep inside her, and she watches me every second of it.

White noise fills my ears, and I lean my forehead against her collarbone, trying to calm my heart, calm my breaths. Her fingers gently play with the hair at the back of my head while my surroundings begin to come back into focus again. I pull back to look at the incredible woman in my lap. The owner of my heart. The mother of my child. She has the most content look on her face.

Sweat drips down the side of my face and collects in a pool on my shoulder. I'm reminded of that night months ago when I watched the drips of water slide down the side of my drink right before I met her for the first time. That night changed my life.

"I liked watching you lose control," Riley says, breaking through the haze.

I let out a chuckle as I fall to my side on the couch and gently pull her with me, cuddling her close to me. I kiss her shoulder, her neck, and her cheek. I'll never get sick of touching her or kissing her.

My mind flits to my family for some reason. I wonder how my parents will react to this. If they'll react at all. I wonder what my brother would have thought if he were here. I wonder if he ever wanted a family of his own.

Suddenly, remembering the cramp she got last time, I prop myself up onto my elbow to look down at her. "Are you okay? I didn't hurt you, did I? Are you cramping?"

"No, I'm not, and no, you didn't." She turns her head slightly to face me and then adds, "And it's not because the orgasm wasn't phenomenal."

I smile down at her before kissing her lips. "Good."

Riley reaches a hand up to my cheek and sighs. "I love you. Is that crazy?"

A warmth spreads throughout my entire body, filling me with a happiness I've never known. "No, it's not crazy." I push some hair off of her forehead, and it feels damp with sweat. "I love you, too." Her smile is soft, and I can't help touching the smooth skin of her lips with my fingers. So soft. "Would you like to shower?"

She nods. "Yes, but maybe in a few more minutes."

I settle back down next to her, holding her close and just enjoying the moment. I think about how quickly things can change. This morning I woke up unhappy and alone, thinking I would never see Riley again. Now she's here in my arms, and everything feels like it's falling into place. I'm happy. *So happy.*

"Did you finish reading the rest of that book?"

She giggles into my chest. "I knew you secretly liked reading it."

I shrug my shoulders, trying to play it off. "Just curious what happens with them."

"Mhmm." She leans back so that she can look at me with a smile. Her eyes are shining brightly with mirth. "No. I didn't finish it, so you can read the rest to me."

I bend my head for another kiss. I can never get enough. "If you insist."

After a few minutes, she sighs. "What are we going to do about Maya?"

Through all of this, I haven't had a chance to really process that part yet. She messed with my life, most likely stole my phone, hurt both Riley and myself, and almost kept me away from my child. Anger starts to replace the joy I felt just a moment ago.

"I'm not sure." I give her body a gentle squeeze. "But I'm sure she stole my phone at work, so that's cause enough for her to be fired."

She nods her head against my chest. Whatever happens with Maya, she won't be coming between us again.

CHAPTER TWENTY-THREE

Riley

Standing in front of the bathroom mirror, I try to adjust my top, moving it this way and that way, trying not to look so giant. It doesn't work, of course. There are only four weeks left until he's due to arrive, and there's no hiding that fact. The knock at my front door brings a smile to my face, and I move as fast as I can to answer it.

"Who's there?" I know exactly who it is, but I can't resist asking anyway.

"It's Jasper."

"Who?" I smile as I open the door. "Oh, I was expecting JD."

He grins, taking a step toward me. "I'll be JD if you

want." Sweeping his eyes over my body, he takes another step inside. "How are you both doing tonight?"

My hands snake up around his neck. "We're doing great. But we missed you."

His eyes immediately soften, and his hands move up to my cheeks, caressing them softly. "I missed both of you, too. You look beautiful."

Jasper and I decided that it would be smart to actually date some more before doing something hasty like moving in together. The past few weeks have been incredible. He picks me up for our dates, or we enjoy dinner together at one of our homes. We even "accidentally" meet up at The Reading Nook, where we sit next to each other, holding hands, silently reading our own books.

Regardless of not living together, we still often end up spending the night at each other's places, then he gets up and goes to work, and I go to hang out at my sister's restaurant. Last night I made him go to Patrick's to play poker, and since it was a late night, he stayed at his own place afterward. I hadn't seen him since yesterday morning, and I felt every second that we were apart.

Really, at this point, I think if he were to suggest that we move in together tonight, I'd have all of my stuff packed and ready to move to his place tomorrow.

"Did you have a good day?" I ask, strumming my fingers up and down his neck.

He smiles down at me. "It definitely just got better."

I hesitate before asking, "Did you call your parents?"

The smile on his face vanishes, and my heart drops. "Yes." He sighs. "They said they'd see us in a few months when dad comes for his hip surgery."

"Oh."

I don't know why disappointment pricks at me. I know

they weren't the most loving and caring parents toward Jasper. I just thought that maybe they'd actually *try* with our baby. He's not going to have any grandparents if they don't care to be in our lives.

I shake my head and try to brush off the feeling. I can't let that bother me. He's going to have two loving parents, my sister and her family, Mia and Kyone and their future kids, and even Patrick, who has become an even better friend to us over the past few weeks. The baby won't need anyone else.

"That's okay, right? By then, he won't just be sleeping all of the time," I say, trying to make light of it.

He gives a head nod, and I tug him down for a kiss, desperate to erase that bit of sadness I see in his eyes.

He leans his forehead against mine and breathes in deeply. "I love you, Riley Shay Brooks."

"I know. And I love you too, Jasper Thomas DeLarouge." I pull back a little to trail my eyes over his handsome face; Rich brown eyes, full lips, and thick dark hair. Every day I make a point to take in his features. Every day I make sure not to take my sight for granted. "Are you ready to go?"

"Yes." He releases my cheeks and grabs my hand. "So, what movie are we seeing again?"

Tonight we are meeting Jordan, Troy, Mia, and Kyone for dinner, and then we're all going to the movies. Little things like that get me excited now, although really, I get excited about doing anything with Jasper.

"Black Widow," I answer.

"Right."

We start walking toward the door, but my steps falter when there is a little flash of light in the corner of my eye. It only lasts for a split second, but anything to do with my eyes has me on edge.

"Are you okay, sweetheart?" Jasper places a hand on my

belly, thinking maybe it's something to do with that.

I give my head a shake. "Yeah. Yeah, I'm okay. It was nothing."

"Are you sure?"

When there are no more flashes, or anything else, I relax and smile up at Jasper. "Yeah. Come on. Let's go."

He keeps his arm around me as we walk to his car. We've met up with the others separately a couple of times but never as one big group. Jasper has made a big effort with all of them and gets along quite well with Troy and Kyone. It makes me so happy when I see him chatting with them and smiling so much.

"What's that look for?" he asks me from the driver's seat.

I take in Jasper's appearance again as he starts the car and glances back at me, waiting for my answer. He's wearing a short sleeve button-down shirt and dark-wash jeans. He said he wants to add more tattoos to his arm to make a sleeve. Maybe the baby's name and birth date mixed in with something else. I still don't think his tattoos match his personality, but I've gotten so used to them and love them so much that I can't imagine him without them. And I love spending time tracing over each of them whenever his shirt is off.

"Just thinking about how perfect you are."

A smirk lifts the side of his mouth, and he faces the road, pulling out into traffic. "Yes, you told me that a few times yesterday morning when I woke you up with my–"

"*Yes.* I remember."

My cheeks heat at the memory. Although I've gotten bigger and feel more awkward trying to maneuver around, the sex between us has gotten even better. Jasper likes to get creative, and we've both discovered that he can be quite dirty at times. He says it's me that has brought it out in him.

Either way, I'm not complaining. I've discovered that I quite like it.

He gives a chuckle and reaches for my hand. "Your cheeks are pink."

"Shush!" I laugh. "Remember when you only said a few words at a time? And they definitely weren't at all dirty or sexual." He grins again as we drive to the restaurant, hand in hand.

The others are already there and seated when we arrive, so we go straight in to join them. Everybody says their hellos as we get settled in.

"How was work?" Mia asks Jasper. "Any twins today?" Since she and Kyone are trying for a baby and Kyone apparently wants to have twins, she's always asking Jasper if he saw any.

"Not today. But tomorrow, I have a patient with triplets coming in. All girls."

Kyone's eyes widen. "Shit. I didn't think about them only being girls. I was aiming for a boy and girl, or both boys."

We all chuckle, and Mia pats him on the chest. "You'll get what you get, honey. And you can't exactly say you want twins and then expect it just to happen."

"Oh, it'll happen, babe. They run in my family."

"That's still not a guarantee," Jasper says to him with a smile as he sips his drink.

"You just wait." Kyone waves his finger around the table. "I'll show you all."

"I meant to ask, Jasper, have you read any of Jeffery Deaver's books?" This comes from Jordan's husband, Troy. Another thing I've learned recently is that Troy enjoys mystery and suspense books as well, but he doesn't usually get a lot of time to read. He and Jasper have been able to bond over it.

The two of them get into a conversation about it, and the rest of us talk about work, kids, and whatever else comes up. Our table is one of the loudest in here while we wait for our meals, and then when our food arrives, everyone digs in with gusto. After finishing off my glass of water, I'm dying to go to the ladies' room.

"I'll come with you," Jordan says, standing and waiting for me to get up.

"'Kay."

When I step out of the cubicle after my twenty-second pee, Jordan is standing against the wall with her arms crossed. "Okay, so tell me what happened to that bitch. I didn't want to ask in front of everyone."

I smile. "I assume you mean Maya?"

"*Yes.* Now tell me she's at least fired or something."

"Yeah, she is." I soap my hands and wash them in cool water as I begin telling her.

Jasper and I – okay, mostly me – had actually come up with this elaborate plan to get back at Maya and get her to admit to what she did. But when I woke up the morning we were supposed to follow through, I just couldn't be bothered with her anymore. Life is too short to go around getting back at people, and at the end of the day, *I* have Jasper.

He did go to his boss and tell him everything that happened, and they ended up searching her desk and finding Jasper's phone, as well as some other items she apparently shouldn't have had. She was let go that same day and hasn't been seen since.

"Good. I'm glad. I seriously wanted to go in there and punch her in the face."

I turn to face her and sigh. "Thanks for always having my back, Jord. I appreciate it."

"Are you kidding me?" Walking over to me, she pulls me

in for a hug and rubs up and down my back. "Of course, I would. Always."

"I miss mom," I say quietly, leaning into her. "I wish she was here to help us both. Although, she'd probably never let our kids go."

"Right?" We both laugh and pull back, facing each other. "And she'd be proud of the woman you've become, Riley-bear."

"She'd be super proud of you, too," I say, trying to wave off tears. "Stop, you're making me cry."

Jordan wipes away a tear as well. "Sorry. Ugh, I've been feeling a little emotional lately, too."

I look her over as she pulls out some paper towel and dabs under her eyes. "Jordan, are you...pregnant?"

She pauses and looks over at me. "I'm not sure, to be honest. I was thinking of taking a test tomorrow."

"What!" I let out a squeal. "Oh my goodness, that's so exciting! I bet Sasha will be ecstatic. She's been wanting a brother or sister forever."

"I know." She smiles. "And our kids will be close in age."

"Yes! And if Mia gets pregnant too, they'll all be close." I let out a happy sigh. "So you're going to take a test tomorrow. Want me to come over for it?"

"Yeah," she says softly. "Yeah, I'd like that."

"Done."

We finish up and head out of the bathroom together. I'm so incredibly happy right now. I'm surrounded by people I love and who love me back. I have a sexy, kind, loving man in my life. And I'll be able to go ahead with my schooling again shortly after the baby is born.

Just as we approach the table, the sudden appearance of more flashes in my eyes, brighter than before, causes me to stumble and reach for a nearby chair.

"Riley!" Jasper calls and is by my side within a few seconds. "What's wrong? Are you okay?"

I squeeze my eyes shut. "There is flashing... in my eyes."

"Flashing? Does it hurt at all?" He rubs his hands up and down my arms in a soothing manner.

"No, no pain. But it doesn't seem right."

"I'll call Patrick, and we'll meet him at the clinic, okay?"

Fear starts to spread throughout me when I think of the possibilities of what it could be. *No.* Please, no. More flashes start, and I cling tightly to Jasper's shirt, needing him close. I hear some staff shuffling around us, trying to see if I'm okay. They probably all assume it's to do with the pregnancy. Jordan and the others are standing close by as well.

"Jasper, what if... what if my sight goes away again? I don't want it to go. I won't be able to look after a baby." I feel tears prickling at the back of my eyes, and it's getting harder to breathe as the panic rises.

"Hey." He reaches up and cups my cheeks, gently brushing his thumbs over my skin. "Try not to worry like that until we know what's going on, okay?" I nod, even though I'm once again thinking about all of the things Pax said to me that day. I won't be able to protect the baby or look after him properly. "And if it does happen," Jasper continues, drawing my attention back. "I'll be with you every step of the way, Riley. We'll get through whatever happens *together*. I promise. You're a strong, amazing woman. You can accomplish so much with or without your sight. Including looking after our baby boy."

The look in his eyes, the steadiness of his voice, and the comfort of his hands have Pax's voice fading away again. It's being replaced with Jasper's words, his strength, and his faith in me. I take a deep breath, trying to calm down.

I can do this.

Whatever happens, I can get through it.

And Jasper will be by my side.

Jasper calls and arranges to meet Patrick at the clinic and then hugs me close as we exit out of the restaurant. The other guys take care of the bill while Jordan and Mia trail out behind us.

"It's going to be okay, Riley," Jordan says.

"No matter what." This comes from Mia. "We're here for you."

I hug them both before getting into the car. Jasper takes my hand in his and kisses my knuckles before placing it on his thigh.

"I've got you," he says and then starts driving to the clinic.

I lean back against the headrest and then close my eyes as more flashes appear.

EPILOGUE

Jasper

"Can you tell me what he looks like?" Riley says from the bathroom.

Leaning on the bed, staring down at our son, Jaxon, I'm still in complete awe. Most days, I can't believe we created such a tiny adorable little person. Eyes with an undetermined color stare back at me as I run my fingers through his soft black hair.

"Not yet," I call back to her. I finish doing the buttons of his new outfit and put on the soft basketball shoes Kyone got for him. "How did I get to be so lucky?" I whisper down at him. He blinks up at me, and I can't resist laying some kisses on his cheek.

There have been quite a few changes over the past little while. Riley moved in with me a few days after that night when she started getting the flashes in her eyes. Neither of us really wanted to be apart anyway, so it made sense, plus it enabled me to help her more.

"All done. Should we see if mommy needs help?" Jaxon makes a cute cooing sound, and I take that as a yes.

"We're ready in here. Do you need any help?" I call out to Riley.

"No," she replies. "I'm used to getting around without my sight."

She comes out of the bathroom slowly and makes her way toward the bed. I grab her hand when she's within reach so she knows where we are, and then I settle her onto my lap. Jaxon is beside us, looking as cute as ever. I straighten his outfit one more time, my heart suddenly pounding against my ribcage.

"Now?" she questions, leaning back into me. I wonder if she can feel the beating of my heart banging against her back. It's like it's trying to escape my chest and bury itself in her.

"Yes."

She reaches up and takes the blindfold off. I hold my breath while she looks down at Jaxon. I had something printed on an outfit for him and told her I wanted to dress him and surprise her with it.

With every passing second that she doesn't say anything, anxiety grows in my gut.

"Yes," she finally says, very quietly.

"Yes?"

"Yes! Of course, yes." She twists around in my lap, wrapping her arms around me in a fierce hug, causing me to fall back onto the bed. I pull her down with me.

She laughs as she lays kisses all over my face. "Of course,

I'll marry you. You're the best person I know."

I roll us over in the opposite direction of Jaxon and trap her beneath me. "Say it again."

"You're the best person I know." She smiles up at me.

I tug on a strand of her hair. "Not that."

"Of course, I'll marry you?"

I slam my mouth down onto hers, kissing her with all the love I feel, pouring my heart into her lips, exploring her mouth for the thousandth time. Nibbling, sucking, stroking her tongue. Never enough.

"Yes, that," I mumble when I finally pull back.

She reaches up to palm my cheek, sighing contentedly, then turns her head toward our baby boy. "Can you believe we made him?"

"I was just thinking that before," I say, idly running my fingers through her hair while looking over at Jaxon. "I'm glad you get to see him, after all."

"Me, too."

That night that we met up with Patrick at the clinic was scary for Riley. My heart broke for her when she thought she would lose her sight again. Just seeing the tears in her eyes and the uncertainty on her face almost did me in. But I had to stay strong for her. I knew that regardless of what happened, I'd be with her every step of the way and would help in any way possible, but I also knew that seeing our baby was something that she had her heart set on. I'm so glad that she was still able to in the end.

Patrick worked quickly to discover what was causing the flashes and, thankfully, was able to fix the issue right away. It was all to do with the accident and side effects of the procedure that was done on her. She needs glasses to read now, but I find them quite sexy. Whenever she's wearing them, I always end up taking them off her so that I can make love to her.

Riley reaches her hand out and strokes Jaxon's cheek with her finger. Jaxon, of course, turns his mouth toward it, thinking it's feeding time again, and we both chuckle at him.

"Do you want to try for another one now?" I'm only joking, but sometimes I just like getting a reaction out of her. I do want a few kids, but I'm willing to wait as long as she wants to.

"Are you crazy? He's not even two months old!" She laughs while squirming to get out from underneath me.

"Come on. They'll be close in age." I lean down and kiss along her jaw.

She tries to push me away. "*Too* close in age."

"Mm, maybe it would be a girl, and he'll look after his little sister."

"Not happening," she says in a breathless tone as I slide my nose along the skin of her neck. "At least not for a few more months."

I pause what I was doing to look down at her. "Really?"

She shrugs and reaches up to trace her fingers over my skin. "I'd like them kind of close-ish together as well. And I know you grew up alone most of the time and would like to have a few kids... I'd like to give you a big family. So, yeah, in maybe six months or so."

I stare down at the woman who brought light into my world, happiness into my life, and a family into my heart. "I'm so glad I found you again," I whisper.

The pure love I see reflected in her eyes tells me that she feels exactly the same as I do about her. I wouldn't even need to hear her words to know them and feel them deep within my soul.

She's about to reply when there's a knock at the door.

"Were you expecting someone?"

I ignore her question and head to the front door while she scoops up Jaxon and follows behind me. Mia stands on the other side with a questioning look on her face. I give the slightest nod and smile.

"Woo! She said yes, guys!" She pushes past me and is followed by Jordan, Sasha, Kyone, Troy, and Patrick, all saying their congratulations as they pass.

"Uh, that was quick." Riley laughs. "It's barely been ten minutes!"

"Well, we all knew when he was planning on doing it, and we knew you'd say yes. We basically just waited out in the hall for as long as we could," Jordan replies. "Now it's time to celebrate!" She steals Jaxon from Riley and walks to the couch so that Sasha can have a hold of her cousin.

I look around the room at the people who have become my family, feeling so blessed to have them all in my life.

Riley's eyes sparkle as she walks up to me and snakes her hands around my neck. "I really love you, you know?"

"Yes. And I love you too, sweetheart."

THE END.

THANK YOU!

Thank you so much for reading Jasper and Riley's story! If you enjoyed it, please consider leaving a rating or review. This helps authors like me to be found :)

Thank you also to my girls, Chloe and Tiffany. You've helped so much along the way and I really appreciate you guys being a sounding board for me!

Also, a big thank you to my beta readers. Love you guys!!

BOOKS BY THIS AUTHOR

Wronged

Remi:
All I wanted was to be away from the limelight, away from my parents. A perfect place where I could live a simple life.

A fresh start.
A small beach town.

That's what I thought I found, until the tortured ocean-colored eyes of the town outcast catch me off guard.

Everyone warns me to stay away from him. They tell me he's a monster.

His eyes tell another story, though, and I need to know what it is. It becomes almost an obsession.

Jacob:
A fresh start in a place where no one knows me…or so I thought. This place has become my own personal Hell.
That is…until her.

She's the only one who doesn't look at me with contempt.

She tries to force her way into my life, but she's better off staying away.

She doesn't deserve this life sentence they've given me.

This book is a raw, emotional, small town romance with dark aspects to it. It contains subject matter that may be upsetting to some readers. It's about finding love under the worst of circumstances and getting second chances in life.
This book is not suitable for a young audience.

Wrecked

Wrecked. It's how Jasmine Delaney found me.

The truth was, I'd been heading down a one-way street to destruction for a long time.

I raced - illegally. I drank - excessively. I slept with women - indiscriminately.

There was no escape in sight.

That is, until I met her. She made me feel whole again, nurturing my heart right along with my soul. But right when I had a reason to be a better man…I did what I always warned her about.

I wrecked it.

She should have stayed away.

Orchids. It's how Campbell Baxter crawled into my heart.

The truth was, I'd been walking down a lonely path for far too long.

I loved - passionately. I gave - freely. I cared - easily.

There was no one worth the risk.

That is, until I met him. He lit my insides on fire, engulfing me in a love like I'd never felt before. But right when everything was in our favor and I'd found what I was looking for...he did what he warned me about.

He wrecked me.

I should have believed him.

CONTACT

Instagram : @author_rin_sher

Facebook: Rin Sher & Rin's Romance Readers

Email: rin.sher.author@gmail.com

TikTok: @rinsherauthor

Printed in Great Britain
by Amazon